# DRUG DANGERS

# The Dangers of Heroin

John Allen

ReferencePoint
Press®

San Diego, CA

30813 9144
R

Reference Point Press®

**For more information, contact:**
ReferencePoint Press, Inc.
PO Box 27779
San Diego, CA 92198
www.ReferencePointPress.com

LIBRARY OF CONGRESS CATALOGING-IN-PUBLICATION DATA

Names: Allen, John, 1957–, author.
Title: The dangers of heroin / by John Allen.
Description: San Diego, CA : ReferencePoint Press, 2017. | Series: Drug
  dangers | Audience: Grade 9 to 12. | Includes bibliographical references
  and index.
Identifiers: | ISBN 9781682820186 (hardback) | ISBN 9781682820193 (eBook)
Subjects: LCSH: heroin abuse--Juvenile literature. | Drug
  abuse--Juvenile literature.

# CONTENTS

# CHAPTER 1: A Drug on the Rise—Again

**P**hilip Seymour Hoffman seemed to have it all. The forty-six-year-old was one of the most versatile film actors of the twenty-first century. He had won an Academy Award for his lead role in the 2005 film *Capote* and had been nominated four other times. He had three children, a thriving career, an affluent lifestyle, and lots of friends. But, as he told a total stranger at the Sundance Film Festival two weeks before he died, he was also a heroin addict.

On February 2, 2014, friends of Hoffman found him dead inside his $10,000-a-month apartment in the West Village of Manhattan. Stuck in his left arm was the needle that had delivered the fatal overdose. The apartment contained seventy plastic bags of heroin, fifty of them still unopened. The little bags were stamped with the words *Ace of Spades* or *Ace of Hearts*, branding them as an especially lethal kind of heroin that is often cut with fentanyl, a potent pain reliever. There were also other drugs scattered inside his home, along with twenty syringes. Hoffman was found to have withdrawn $1,200 from an ATM down the street in order to buy more heroin the night before. Then he had gone back to his apartment to resume his binge, knowing full well the danger involved. As he had told some friends at Christmas, "If I don't stop I know I'm going to die."[1]

> "If I don't stop [using heroin] I know I'm going to die."[1]
>
> —Actor Philip Seymour Hoffman.

## Easy Availability

The coroner found that Hoffman died from a mixture of drugs, with heroin being the main culprit. In addition to heroin, the coroner found cocaine, benzodiazepines (tranquilizers), and amphetamines in his system. Experts noted that an addict like Hoffman, who was accustomed to mixing drugs, probably was not aware of the stress this placed on his respiratory system and on his ability to breathe. Thus, the actor's death was ruled an accident—despite his own foreboding about the dangers of heroin.

Hoffman's case demonstrates the wide availability of heroin on US streets. It also shows how easy it is for recovering addicts to

*Philip Seymour Hoffman (pictured in 2013) was an Academy Award–winning actor who had family, friends, and a thriving career. He was also a heroin addict—and his addiction killed him.*

have a relapse. A few days after his death, Manhattan police arrested four people in connection with Hoffman's heroin purchases. One man, a musician acquaintance named Robert Aaron, had Hoffman's number stored in his cell phone. A search of Aaron's apartment uncovered nearly three hundred small bags of heroin like those found in the actor's home. For addicts with a ready source of cash, supply is not a problem. A heroin user himself, Aaron refused to accept blame for Hoffman's death. "He was an adult," Aaron said. "He'd been doing it a while, he knew what he was up against. Nobody killed him."[2]

## Grim Reputation, Grim Statistics

Heroin abuse has gone from being mostly a minority, inner-city problem in the 1960s and 1970s to a white, suburban problem today. Experts on drug abuse suggest that the demographic most at risk today for heroin use is young suburban adults. In 2014 the journal *JAMA Psychiatry* published a survey of nine thousand drug-treatment patients across the nation. The study found that 90 percent of those receiving treatment for heroin use were young white men and women, with an average age of twenty-three.

Statistics showing the increase in heroin addiction in the United States are shocking. The National Survey on Drug Use and Health found that between 2007 and 2012, heroin dependence nearly doubled among young adults. In roughly the same period the number of first-time users also exploded, swelling from 90,000 to 169,000. The survey also found that in 2012 about 670,000 Americans reported taking heroin during the previous year. Moreover, an increasing number of users do not survive the drug. According to the Centers for Disease Control and Prevention, the rate of heroin-related overdose deaths almost quadrupled from 2002 to 2013. More than 8,200 users died from overdose in 2013 alone.

Surprising also are the locales in the grip of heroin abuse. New Hampshire, for example, with its rolling green hills dotted with red barns and its neat small towns lined with family-owned shops and

# Fentanyl: A Deadly Synthetic Painkiller

In his job for a funeral home in Manchester, New Hampshire, Joel Murphy has too often performed the grim duty of picking up the corpses of young overdose victims. Usually they are males in their twenties, still wearing ball caps over their close-cropped hair, their bodies shriveled by drug use. Heroin and pain pills are often the culprits, but increasingly these young men are found to have died from using a synthetic painkiller called fentanyl. Murphy knows the dangers because his own son has battled addiction to fentanyl for several years.

Fentanyl was first synthesized in the 1960s. In the mid-1990s, amid the explosion of opioid painkillers, drug companies promoted fentanyl as a treatment for severe pain, such as that experienced by cancer patients. Fentanyl is up to fifty times stronger than heroin and can be produced more cheaply. Its profitability has made it a fixture on American streets. Mexican cartels can buy a kilo of illegal fentanyl from China for less than $5,000 and then sell it wholesale to buyers in the United States for as much as $90,000. Cutting fentanyl with powdered sugar or some other substance can swell profits even more. Overdose often results when users inject heroin that, unbeknownst to them, has been mixed with fentanyl to create a deadly cocktail. Just two milligrams of fentanyl—equal in weight to six grains of salt—can end a user's life almost instantaneously. In New Hampshire alone, 283 fentanyl-linked deaths occurred in 2015 compared to 88 from heroin.

businesses, seems the essence of placid New England. Nonetheless, pollsters for the February 2016 New Hampshire presidential primary were startled to find that the chief concern for citizens there is not the economy or jobs but drugs. The Granite State has one of the highest per capita rates of heroin addiction in the country. About one person in New Hampshire each day dies as a result of opioid (drugs related to the opium poppy) overdose, including heroin and prescription painkillers. Overdose victims are found in almost all demographics. The situation is often referred to locally as an epidemic. "Our families are dying," says Susan Allen-Samuel, whose son has battled back from heroin addiction. "What's going on in our community is a war."[3]

## Heroin's Path to the Suburbs

The new face of heroin abuse in America—young, suburban, and increasingly female—owes its beginnings to a wave of addiction to prescription painkillers. The 2014 *JAMA Psychiatry* survey found that three out of four heroin users first started taking prescription opioid drugs like OxyContin or Vicodin. This group of pain medications came to prominence in the 1990s, when large pharmaceutical companies launched vigorous campaigns to promote the drugs. Doctors by the thousands were treated to expensive junkets and fed misleading information about the pills, with their risk of addiction often downplayed. Sales reps for the drug companies earned bonuses in the millions for persuading physicians to prescribe the new painkillers. As the numbers of prescriptions rose, the instances of abuse and addiction exploded. Deaths from overdose of prescription painkillers like OxyContin and Percocet more than quadrupled from 1999 to 2011.

"Our families are dying. What's going on in our community is a war."[3]

—Susan Allen-Samuel, whose son has battled back from heroin addiction.

The wide availability of prescription painkillers in suburbs and small towns across America led bored, anxious, or thrill-seeking young people to open the medicine cabinet and experiment with the drugs. Some, of course, began using painkillers for legitimate reasons—to help them recover from auto accidents, job-related mishaps, or sports injuries. Once users were hooked on pain meds, however, the move to heroin was often a matter of simple economics. Whereas one OxyContin pill costs about eighty dollars on the street, a single hit of heroin averages about ten dollars and can be found for as little as four dollars. Even teenagers in economically depressed small towns can afford regular purchases of heroin.

A July 2012 study published in the *New England Journal of Medicine* further illustrates how painkiller addiction fueled the heroin addiction epidemic in America. The study included more than twenty-five hundred patients in treatment centers from thirty-nine states. Of the patients being treated for heroin addiction, 76 percent got started by taking prescription pain pills. Of those, more than 90 percent admitted there were two main reasons they switched from painkillers to heroin: 1) the painkillers got too expensive, and 2) they became too hard to locate. When the painkillers to which many thousands were addicted were no longer available, desperate addicts had to find a replacement quickly.

Other factors also contributed to the increase in heroin use. Concern about the overprescription of pain pills produced new laws that finally began to limit their circulation; this in turn pushed users to heroin. Similarly, efforts by the US Food and Drug Administration (FDA) and drug companies to curb the abuse of prescription painkillers actually resulted in heroin's abuse. For example, in 2010 the FDA authorized a new chemical formulation for OxyContin that makes the drug more difficult to crush, break, or dissolve and also causes it to form a viscous gel that resists injection when mixed in a syringe. These changes had the perverse effect of turning users toward heroin as a replacement.

In addition, once marijuana legalization took hold in the United States and more potent strains of pot became available in many states, Mexican drug cartels—which had formerly sold marijuana— now found that market increasingly taken over by US growers whose products are regulated and reliable in quality. The cartels therefore switched to trafficking in heroin, which is also less difficult to deliver and conceal.

The flood of cheap heroin soon reached suburbs and small towns, where young opioid addicts made up a ready market. Widespread use and familiarity soon began to ease some of the fears attached to the drug. For growing numbers of young people, heroin was no longer an object of dread—associated with inner-city junkies and the high-profile deaths of rock stars like Jim

# Rising Levels of Heroin Dependence and Heroin-Related Deaths

Heroin abuse and its deadly consequences are a growing problem in the United States. Between 2002 and 2013 the rate of abuse of heroin or addiction to the drug per one thousand people doubled. The rate of heroin-related overdose deaths also soared, rising 286 percent between those same years.

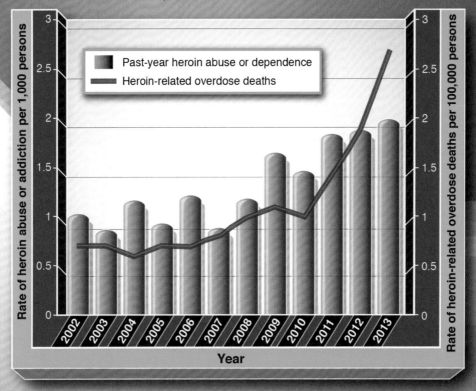

Source: Lindsey Cook, "The Heroin Epidemic, in 9 Graphs," *U.S. News & World Report,* August 19, 2015. www.usnews.com.

Morrison and Kurt Cobain—but merely a fairly inexpensive means to escape oneself for a while. Theodore Cicero, vice chairman of psychiatric research at the Washington University School of Medicine in St. Louis, Missouri, notes how the drug has broken through old boundaries. "The stigma is going away as people begin to see heroin used by friends or acquaintances that they didn't think would be taking it,"[4] he says. Nonetheless, with addiction rates on the rise, the bleak reality of heroin abuse seems sure to reassert itself in the public mind.

# An Alternative to Morphine

Ironically, heroin was originally developed as a nonaddictive alternative to other pain medications, particularly morphine. Around 1810 morphine was found to be the active pain-relieving ingredient in opium. German chemists were able to isolate it by dissolving opium in acid and then neutralizing the product with ammonia. Physicians seized on morphine as a wonder drug for its ability to treat severe pain, such as during surgical operations or from traumatic injuries. However, morphine proved to be toxic and highly addictive—as shown by the terrible rates of addiction among Civil War soldiers who were treated with the drug for battlefield wounds.

Spurred by doctors' reports, the quest was on for a safer alternative to morphine. In 1874 a London chemist named C.R. Alder Wright combined morphine with acids to make a painkiller that was much like heroin. At the end of the nineteenth century, Felix Hoffmann, a German researcher, developed an opium-based pain reliever with a similar molecular structure to that of morphine but supposedly without its addictive properties. In 1898 the Bayer Company of Germany began producing the new medicine for sale, calling it Heroin—probably from the German *heroisch* for its heroic effectiveness—and marketing it as a safe, non–habit-forming replacement for morphine. The new painkiller had twice the potency of morphine, and it took effect more rapidly. Heroin quickly became a sensation, as popular as the pain relievers seen on television ads today.

> "The stigma is going away as people begin to see heroin used by friends or acquaintances that they didn't think would be taking it."[4]
>
> —Theodore Cicero, vice chairman of psychiatric research at the Washington University School of Medicine.

In the United States, drug companies sold heroin over the counter in special drug kits, complete with hypodermic needles for administering the medicine. Heroin, like other opiates, was used to treat children and adults for a range of ailments, from tuberculosis and depression to coughs and colds. Physicians discovered, however, that heroin was even more addictive than morphine and thus had no medical value. With the Harrison Act of 1914, the United States began to regulate the drug with taxes. Six years later Congress made it illegal to manufacture, import, and/or possess heroin, even for medicinal use, bringing an end to over-the-counter sales. By then the number of heroin addicts in the United States was estimated to be almost two hundred thousand.

Succeeding decades saw heroin go underground as a street drug. Its use was confined mainly to urban areas. In the 1940s and 1950s many high-profile jazz musicians got hooked on heroin, including the great bebop saxophonist Charlie Parker, who lost his life to the drug. Heroin overdose also claimed the lives of celebrated performers of the rock era, such as singer Janis Joplin and actor John Belushi. By the 1970s heroin was notorious as a scourge of the inner cities and housing projects in America, to be gradually replaced by crack cocaine and other street drugs. Easy availability led to the resurgence of heroin use seen today in small towns and suburbs. In recent years heroin overdose has once more made national headlines, as with Philip Seymour Hoffman's case and the death in 2013 of *Glee* actor Cory Monteith from a mixture of heroin and alcohol.

# The Chemistry of Heroin

The thriving market for heroin, one of the most lethal narcotics in the world, owes much to the euphoric rush users feel upon injecting the drug. This effect comes from morphine, the active ingredient in heroin and other opiates. The chemical name for heroin is diacetylmorphine, which basically means it is morphine combined with acetyls, or acetic acids. A single molecule of heroin consists of twenty-one atoms of carbon, twenty-three atoms of hydrogen, one atom of nitrogen, and five atoms of oxygen. Once heroin is injected and reaches the brain, it quickly sheds the acetyl groups in its chemical makeup and metabolizes into morphine.

The molecular structure of morphine mimics that of a class of chemicals called endorphins, which the brain produces naturally. Endorphins flood into a person's system when the body feels pain or stress. The chemicals cut off pain signals between nerve cells to induce a painkilling, or analgesic, effect. Molecules of morphine in heroin attach to the brain's nerve endings just like endorphins, causing the user to experience a powerful euphoria or rush of pleasure. They also induce effects lasting for several hours, such as relaxation, drowsiness, and lack of mental focus.

## Where Heroin Comes From

Heroin comes from a flower often grown for its beauty. The opium poppy has the Latin name *Papaver somniferum*, which translates as "sleep-producing poppy." Heroin and other opiates are derived from the resin of the poppy plant. When petals of the brightly colored poppy flower fall away, they reveal a rounded seed pod.

*Heroin comes from the flowers known as opium poppies (pictured). Once the flower's petals fall away, a rounded seed pod remains, and within that pod is the thick, milky sap that makes up a crude form of opium.*

This pod contains a thick, milky sap—the crude form of opium. To extract this substance, the pod is slit with a curved knife, causing the sap to ooze out and thicken into a brownish-black gum.

The gumlike opium is boiled in water with lime until a white layer of morphine forms on the surface. The morphine is scraped off and repeatedly boiled and filtered with ammonia, leaving a brown paste. The paste is emptied into molds and dried in the sun until it hardens to the consistency of modeling clay. Now it is ready to be purified through a series of steps in a laboratory, however makeshift. First, the morphine is heated with an acid for six hours, forming diacetylmorphine. Next, impurities are removed by heating the solution with water and chloroform. This solution is replaced with sodium carbonate, which causes the heroin to condense and sink to the bottom of the container. Then the heroin is filtered out with charcoal and purified further with alcohol. In a fourth step, the alcohol solution is heated until it evaporates, leaving a fine white powder—pure heroin, or number four heroin, as traffickers call it. This last step, which includes ether and hydrochloric acid, involves considerable risk of explosion should the ether ignite.

The opium poppy grows best in warm, dry climates. Traditionally most of the world's opium poppies are grown in the so-called Golden Triangle, a mountainous region that includes territory in Myanmar (formerly Burma), Laos, and Thailand. By the start of the twenty-first century, Afghanistan had surpassed Southeast Asia as the leading producer of opium poppies, and it remains the world's chief source. However, a 2015 United Nations report noted that cultivation in the Golden Triangle has tripled since 2006, largely due to increased trafficking of opium and heroin in China. Opium is refined into heroin in scattered laboratories in Myanmar, Hong Kong, and Thailand and then packaged in bulk shipments of 88 to 220 pounds (40 to 100 kg) for distribution throughout Southeast Asia and China.

# Heroin in the United States

Most of the heroin sold in the United States comes from Colombia and Mexico, with Colombian heroin found mainly east of the Mississippi River and Mexican heroin to the west. To feed their distribution systems, growers in these countries have devoted thousands

# Targeting Middle America

Until his arrest by DEA agents, Gerardo A. Vargas served as a drug mule—a courier who smuggled powdered heroin from Uruapan, Mexico, into the United States. His overseers forced him to swallow seventy-one pellets of heroin, each tightly wrapped in waxed paper and latex. Vargas had to abide by strict rules to complete his mission. No drinking soda or orange juice, whose acids might dissolve the pellet wrapping. No eating until after the goal is reached. Above all, stick to the plan, and stay away from certain airports and other risky areas. The seventy-one pellets represented a potentially big score—a complete kilo, a bit more than two pounds. On the streets of Dayton, Ohio, Vargas's ultimate destination, this heroin could be sold as thirty thousand separate hits at ten dollars apiece.

Today Mexican heroin cartels are experiencing a bonanza, taking advantage of the shift from pain pills to heroin in many suburbs and small towns in America. Their ability to manufacture high-quality powdered heroin, instead of the crude black tar heroin of years past, has opened lucrative new markets for their product. The powder takes up less room and so can be smuggled more easily. Diluting the heroin makes it even more profitable. The cartels can afford to pay smugglers like Vargas up to $6,000 for a successful mission. Like aggressive businesses the world over, the cartels are constantly testing new marketing ploys. When they first targeted Dayton, for example, they offered free sample hits of powdered heroin to buyers of pot or crack cocaine—anything to snare a repeat customer.

of acres of land to the cultivation of opium poppies. The Mexican cartels are the fastest-growing source of heroin in the United States. According to the *Washington Post*, in 2014 Mexican traffickers smuggled an estimated 225,000 pounds (102,058 kg) of heroin into the United States. A single kilo (about two pounds) of heroin is enough for nearly thirty thousand doses, or hits, each of which costs an American user ten dollars or more on the street—representing at least a tenfold increase in value from its manufactured state. "Mexican cartels have overtaken the U.S. heroin trade, imposing an almost corporate discipline," writes *Washington Post* reporter Todd C. Frankel. "They grow and process the drug themselves, increasingly replacing their traditional black tar [variety] with an innovative high-quality powder with mass market appeal."[5]

On American streets, heroin goes by many names, including smack, junk, scag, horse, dog, dope, girl, Big H, white, tar, chiva, hell dust, and brown sugar. To maximize profits, heroin sold on the street is often cut, or diluted, with other ingredients such as powdered milk, starch, sugar, and flour. It may be mixed with another pain medication, such as acetaminophen, a painkilling drug found in over-the-counter pain relievers, or fentanyl, a strong analgesic drug. Some heroin is even mixed with chalk or concrete dust.

Nonetheless, the overall potency of heroin generally has increased. While street heroin in the 1970s and 1980s tended to be 10 percent pure, today it averages 30 percent purity nationwide and often is as much as 70 percent pure, according to US Drug Enforcement Administration (DEA) reports. This is another factor contributing to the rise in heroin addiction and incidents of overdose. Since heroin sales are illegal and occur in the shadows, the street buyer is at the mercy of the seller, with no guarantees about what he or she is buying. The wide variations in purity for heroin sold on the street make the drug even more dangerous and unpredictable. If heroin is mixed with another powerful narcotic, the risks of overdose are greatly increased. Users accustomed to a lower level of potency can face deadly consequences should they suddenly encounter a purer form.

> "Mexican cartels have overtaken the U.S. heroin trade, imposing an almost corporate discipline."[5]
>
> —Todd C. Frankel, reporter for the *Washington Post.*

## Focus on Awareness and Treatment

The disturbing increase in heroin use not only in the United States but worldwide has authorities scrambling for answers. Of particular concern is the drug's recent outbreak among young people. Substance abuse experts say young people at risk of heroin addiction must be made aware of the dangers and provided with counseling and treatment centers should problems develop. The shocking frequency with which heroin-related deaths occur today must serve as a spur to action.

# CHAPTER 2: The Effects of Heroin Abuse

**E**than Romeo was twenty years old when he first took heroin. The Ware, Massachusetts, man began smoking marijuana at age eleven, and throughout his teens he frequently snorted cocaine and took pain pills. Nonetheless, the thought of using a needle had always convinced him to stay away from heroin. That is, until one night when Romeo was with a friend and fellow user, and the pair's growing addiction to OxyContin, a strong pain reliever, had both of them feeling nauseated, listless, and completely exhausted. To counter what Romeo called their dope sickness, they decided to give heroin a try.

They drove to the house of a dealer in the nearby town of South Hadley. The dealer and a former girlfriend of Romeo's had all the paraphernalia set up on the dining room table. She went first. Watching the needle enter her vein, Romeo realized it was the first time he had ever seen anyone shoot up. Next up was Romeo's buddy. When Romeo's turn came, the dealer walked him through the process, including finding a good vein and ensuring that the needle was clean. Shortly after the needle penetrated his skin, Romeo experienced a rush like nothing he had known in all his years of drug use. This lasted for perhaps thirty seconds, followed by a euphoric high that would continue for several hours. It took only twenty minutes, however, for Romeo to start craving more heroin. He wanted to reproduce that initial feeling. "I was ready to go," he says. "From the very first time I shot heroin I immediately fell in love."[6]

## The Initial Rush

The overpowering allure of heroin is the rapid rush of pleasurable sensations that the drug produces. Users report a wave of euphoria, followed by a warm flushing of the skin and a dry mouth.

Injecting heroin ensures that these effects are more immediate. First-time users also may experience nausea from heroin's potent kick. Sebastian, now middle-aged, first tried heroin at a party when he was nineteen. With a half dozen others looking on—and a plastic garbage pail placed nearby—he received an injection and then leaned back in an armchair. He recalls the drug's powerful effect:

> Lots of warmth. Different waves of warmth around my body, and then all of a sudden I hurled into the bin, much to the laughter of everyone around me. Then I sat back and the rush turned up and oh my god, it was good. It was very good. I didn't know that I could have that much sensation in my body. I didn't know that I was capable of feeling that much enjoyment. The initial rush lasted about 20 minutes then there were six to eight hours where I was very relaxed, calm, and had a sense of heightened well-being.[7]

Once the euphoria fades, the user's arms and legs grow heavy and he or she becomes drowsy. A period of pleasurable numbness and relaxation sets in for several hours. Some users describe feelings of calmness and safety, an escape from pain, depression, loneliness, or anxiety. The user may seem to be floating in a disconnected dream. Breathing and heart rate slow down, and the user's mental faculties cloud over and grow distorted. He or she becomes drowsy and may drop off to sleep—an experience referred to as nodding.

## A Dreadful Experience

Other first-time users find shooting up heroin to be extremely unpleasant. Besides the uncontrolled nausea, they may have difficulty breathing, suffer outbreaks of severe itching, and run the risk of choking on their own vomit. One bad experience can cause a user to swear off heroin for life. The risk of overdose, and the anxiety of

# The Health Effects of Heroin

Heroin is a highly addictive opioid, or narcotic. It is made from morphine, which is a natural substance refined from sap extracted from the seed pod of the Asian opium poppy plant. Users of heroin experience a variety of health effects ranging from dry mouth and clouded thinking to collapsed veins and liver or kidney disease. When combined with alcohol, heroin use can result in death.

## Possible Health Effects

| | |
|---|---|
| Short-term | Euphoria; warm flushing of skin; dry mouth; heavy feeling in the hands and feet; clouded thinking; alternate wakeful and drowsy states; itching; nausea; vomiting; slowed breathing and heart rate. |
| Long-term | Collapsed veins; abscesses (tissue swollen with pus); infection of the lining and valves in the heart; constipation and stomach cramps; liver or kidney disease; pneumonia. |
| Other health-related issues | Pregnancy: miscarriage, low birth weight, neonatal abstinence syndrome. Risk of HIV, hepatitis, and other infectious diseases from shared needles. |
| In combination with alcohol | Dangerous slowdown of heart rate and breathing, coma, death. |
| Withdrawal symptoms | Restlessness, muscle and bone pain, insomnia, diarrhea, vomiting, cold flashes with goose bumps ("cold turkey"), leg movements. |

Source: National Institute on Drug Abuse, "Commonly Abused Drugs Charts," April 2016. www.drugabuse.gov.

confronting that risk, may also be a problem. A user has no idea what might be mixed with the heroin he or she buys on the street or is administered in a drug house. Purity levels are unpredictable, although in the United States they have been steadily on the rise. A dealer may offer wildly varied types and strengths of heroin from week to week. Heroin mixed with a painkiller such as OxyContin or the even more potent fentanyl can lead to deadly consequences. The user's lips and nails can turn blue, breathing can slow perilously, skin may become clammy, and he or she may be prey to violent spasms and seizures, leading to coma and possible death.

The sleep-inducing effect of heroin is also one of its main hazards. "Heroin makes someone calm and a little bit sleepy," says Dr. Karen Drexler, director of the addiction psychiatry training program at Emory University, "but if you take too much then you can fall asleep, and when you are asleep your respiratory drive shuts down. Usually when you are sleeping, your body naturally remembers to breathe. In the case of a heroin overdose, you fall asleep and essentially your body forgets."[8]

> "Usually when you are sleeping, your body naturally remembers to breathe. In the case of a heroin overdose, you fall asleep and essentially your body forgets."[8]
>
> —Dr. Karen Drexler, director of the addiction psychiatry training program at Emory University.

Overdosing on heroin can also reduce blood pressure drastically and lead to heart failure. Injecting heroin greatly increases the risk of infectious endocarditis, which is basically an infection of the heart's inner lining and heart valves. It can trigger an arrhythmia, or irregular heartbeat, affecting blood flow to the organs. It can result in pulmonary edema, which also restricts blood flow and causes blood to back up into the veins. This condition limits normal oxygen flow through the lungs and can lead to shortness of breath, heart attack, or kidney failure. Studies indicate that dying instantly from taking heroin is not common, occurring only in about 14 percent of deaths related to heroin use. Nevertheless, taking heroin even one time is like playing Russian roulette.

Ignoring warnings about the dangers of addiction and overdose, Sebastian injected heroin three more times within a month of his first use. Quitting at that point was hard for him, but fortunately he was able to walk away from the drug. Many beginning users, like Ethan Romeo, are not so fortunate. Unlike Sebastian, Romeo slid into the routine of a full-blown heroin addict. "I knew then and there that my life had changed forever," says Romeo, "and I would forever be addicted to a needle."[9]

# The Trouble with Needles

Many users, like Romeo and Sebastian, take heroin through the traditional process of injecting it into a vein in the arm, or mainlining, as it is called. This method delivers the most intense rush from the least amount of drug—and also presents the greatest danger of overdose. Heroin can also be injected under the skin, called skin-popping, or into a muscle. To prepare a fifteen-dollar chunk of black tar heroin for intravenous use, it is usually heated, or cooked. The brownish, faintly vinegary chunk is placed in a spoon and then a small amount of water is added with a syringe. A lighter is used to heat the spoon from the bottom and dissolve the chunk. Once the heroin is completely dissolved into liquid, a rolled ball of cotton is dropped into the solution until it swells like a sponge. Then the syringe is used to suck the liquid heroin out of the cotton, which acts as a filter for any germs and dirt particles.

The target area for injection is swabbed with alcohol to steril-ize it. A rubber hose or shoestring may be used as a tourniquet to tie off the arm and cause veins to bulge, making them easier to hit with the needle. Novice users concentrate on veins at the

*A heroin user prepares for a fix by heating and dissolving a chunk of black tar heroin mixed with water. Once the drug is fully liquefied, it will be prepared for injection.*

# An Antidote for Heroin Overdose

One morning in March 2016, police in Bethlehem, Pennsylvania, responded to an all-too-typical 911 call. A young man had overdosed on heroin. Officers Robert Corsi and Jeremy Rimmer arrived to find the subject unconscious, with his lips turning blue and no vital signs. In the past this story would inevitably have had a tragic end. But instead Corsi and Rimmer were able to offer emergency medical procedures on site to save the victim. Revived, almost miraculously, the young man was whisked away for treatment at a nearby hospital. He owes his life to the officers' training and to a medication called naloxone.

Naloxone, also known by its brand name, Narcan, is essentially an antidote for heroin overdose. It is formulated to counter the effects of overdose from opioids such as heroin, morphine, and prescription painkillers. It prevents the opioids from binding to certain receptors in the brain that control respiratory functions. The Bethlehem officers relied on their training to administer an injection of naloxone from a pocket-sized device. The device, which the FDA approved for emergency use in April 2014, is also recommended for family members and caregivers of any-one at risk for opioid abuse. With naloxone now widely available, heroin overdose need no longer be a death sentence. "The primary job of any law enforcement officer is the preservation of human life," says Bethlehem police chief Mark DiLuzio. "Officers across the US do this every day in many different ways. Naloxone is now one of these many ways."

Quoted in Tony Rhodin, "Bethlehem Police Use Naloxone to Save Overdose Victim, Chief Says," LehighValleyLive, March 29, 2016. www.lehighvalleylive.com.

bend of the arm, but hardened addicts may seek unused veins on the wrist and back of the hand. Once the needle pierces the vein and heroin enters the user's system, the euphoric payoff occurs almost instantaneously, as the drug metabolizes into morphine in the brain. In an attempt to increase the effect, some users inject a speedball, which is a mixture of heroin and cocaine.

Use of needles to obtain the desired rush carries with it many risks besides overdose. For example, heroin users often share a needle when shooting up. This means each user is letting bodily fluids from the other user into his or her own bloodstream. This increases the chance of contracting HIV, the virus that produces AIDS. It also presents the danger of getting hepatitis, a disease that inflames the liver and weakens the body's ability to reject toxins. With the increased intravenous (IV) use of heroin in recent years, cases of hepatitis B and C have also grown.

Another risk is infection of subcutaneous tissues—below the skin's surface—from a dirty needle and generally unsanitary surroundings. This can lead to a serious bacterial infection of the skin called cellulitis. It can also cause the formation of an abscess, which is an inflamed pocket filled with pus that hardens in red streaks and blotches around the injection site. Without treatment, these conditions can destroy tissues, warrant amputation, or even become life-threatening infections. IV use of heroin also damages the affected blood veins in various ways. Regular users may see their veins collapse, harden, or become badly scarred—the notorious tracks of heroin addicts. Damage to veins can restrict blood flow and prevent scarred areas from healing. Even when using the smallest possible needles, such as syringes for diabetics, and varying injection sites, IV heroin users inevitably inflict harm on their veins and capillaries.

As users become hooked on heroin, they begin to pay less attention to injecting the drug with care. Poor technique in using the needle causes further problems. "As veins are exhausted, more dangerous sites are used," says Meg Thomas, a doctor in Swindon, England, who has treated many IV heroin users. Thomas observes that injecting into the femoral vein in the upper thigh and pelvic region can cause deep vein thrombosis, or blood clots in the legs, as well as arterial bleeding and restricted blood flow. Injections into the neck can harm major nerves and blood vessels. Some female users risk mastitis—inflammation of the breast—by inserting the needle into breast veins. Desperate male users may seek out veins in the penis. As Thomas notes, "the disinhibiting [freeing] effect of the drug leads to a bravado approach where knowledge of safe injecting is ignored."[10]

# Sniffing or Snorting Heroin

One reason for heroin's growth as a recreational drug is that newer forms can be taken in ways that do not involve a needle. The availability of heroin as a fine powder enables users to snort it or smoke it. Young adults in the suburbs, scarcely aware of the dangerous purity of the heroin they purchase at a discount, tell themselves—mistakenly—that smoking or snorting the drug is less addictive. They may proceed to use heroin even more recklessly, in ways that actually increase their chances of becoming hooked or overdosing.

The appeal of sniffing or snorting heroin is its ease. Unlike IV injection or smoking, these methods require very little in the way of paraphernalia. Sniffing heroin means to inhale it only into the lower part of the nostril. Snorting involves sucking the drug deeper into the upper level of the nostril. A straw or rolled-up dollar bill is the tool used for snorting heroin. Some users snort alternate lines of heroin and cocaine, a practice known as crisscrossing. Some even use a nasal spray bottle to sniff liquefied heroin, which is called shabanging.

Inhaling heroin does not produce an instantaneous rush like mainlining. Instead, the heroin takes about five minutes to be absorbed into the small blood vessels in the nose and lungs. Once in the bloodstream, it moves quickly into the brain and produces a milder euphoria. Although the chance of overdose from sniffing or snorting heroin is reduced, there is still considerable risk of a deadly result. Those who sniff or snort the drug are more likely to be occasional users, and they may be poor judges of a dose's potency or of their own tolerance. Asthma sufferers who sniff heroin can trigger serious attacks that require immediate medical care.

Although sniffing or snorting the drug eliminates many of the dangers of using a needle, these methods pose their own hazards. Repeated snorting of heroin can break down the lining of the nostril, resulting in nasal bleeding. Sharing a straw or rolled-up bill with someone who is bleeding in this way subjects the user to possible infection with the hepatitis C virus. "Obviously, the more drugs you put in [the nose], the more you're going to irritate your [nasal] vascular wall, and that's going to result in a little bleeding in the nose," according to Dr. Thomas Kresina, a spokesperson for the National Institute on Drug Abuse. "Then that blood goes on the instrument you use [to sniff or snort], and you transfer that to the next person. That's where the risk occurs."[11]

# Chasing the Dragon

Another way to take heroin is to smoke it. Smoking the drug delivers heroin to the brain more quickly than sniffing or snorting. Heroin, usually of the brown tar variety, is placed on a sheet of tinfoil or some other material that heats up rapidly. A flame is applied to the bottom of the tinfoil, causing the heroin to vaporize. The user then inhales the smoke and vapors through a straw or tube, a technique called chasing the dragon. Heroin can also be smoked in a pipe, a bong (or water pipe), or mixed into a marijuana joint or regular cigarette. Some users even heat heroin in a teapot on the stove and inhale the drug through the spout.

Susan, a recovering addict in Cork, Ireland, recalls the attraction of smoking heroin as a teenager. "When I was smoking it every day I loved it," she admits, "I loved the whole thing, I loved the brown [liquid] running down the foil, I just loved everything: the smell, the taste, there's not even a big smell off it, but I'd sit at

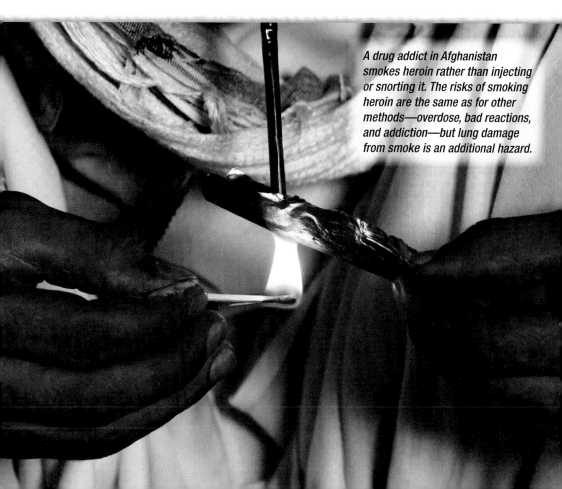

*A drug addict in Afghanistan smokes heroin rather than injecting or snorting it. The risks of smoking heroin are the same as for other methods—overdose, bad reactions, and addiction—but lung damage from smoke is an additional hazard.*

home on my own, smoking all day and hiding bags, putting bags away for later."[12] Not long afterward, Susan somehow survived falling off a three-story building while in a heroin-induced stupor.

The risks of smoking heroin, besides the obvious ones of overdose, bad reactions, and addiction, are the same associated with smoking any toxic substance, including damaging the lungs and breathing passages. Smoking the drug can also cause leukoencephalopathy, an infection of the white matter of the brain. Early symptoms include slurred speech and problems with walking. If not treated promptly, the disease can advance into cognitive decay, vision loss, speech problems, and loss of coordination.

The slang term *chasing the dragon* dates to the 1920s, and the smoking of heroin and opium in China and other Asian locales. The term refers to the way the smoker keeps moving the liquefied heroin around the tinfoil or heated surface to keep it from congealing into an unusable mass. However, chasing the dragon has also come to represent the heroin user's obsessive and often deadly quest for the perfect high. The user feels certain that the next dose will sweep him or her into some imagined ecstasy that never quite arrives. This is because repeated use and the resulting tolerance to the drug dulls its positive effects—and ushers in many negative ones. "Heroin has amazing PR [public relations]," says recovering addict Sarah Beach. "It is an absolute bait-and-switch of a drug. For a few weeks, maybe, you feel better than you've ever felt in your life, but after that it stops feeling good at all. You now have to use it to avoid the unbelievably horrific withdrawal symptoms."[13] When this happens, the user chases the elusive dragon even more obsessively in an attempt to go beyond—or simply recapture—the initial thrill. In the grip of the drug, a heroin smoker may turn to the needle for a more intense high. This is the psychological trap of heroin abuse.

# Physical and Mental Problems

Apart from full-blown addiction, regular users of heroin can experience a variety of serious physical and mental problems. Chronic users often suffer from insomnia, cold sweats, and persistent constipation. Frequently they have sunken eyes, rotten teeth, and

# Deadly Combinations

On July 13, 2013, Canadian actor Cory Monteith of the popular television series *Glee* died in a hotel room in downtown Vancouver, British Columbia. The thirty-one-year-old was found to have indulged a deadly mixture of heroin and alcohol. A used hypodermic needle, a spoon with heroin residue, and two empty champagne bottles were discovered near the actor's body. Monteith, who had a history of drug abuse and several stints in rehab, paid the price for recklessly combining substances, a habit all too common among hardened users. In Monteith's case, the deadening effect of heroin, which is a depressant that slows the heartbeat, was made worse by adding alcohol, another depressant. Together the two drugs stopped Monteith's heart. "This is known as a synergistic effect," explains Lawrence Kobilinsky, a professor at New York City's John Jay College of Criminal Justice. "One plus one equals three." Even a milder dose of heroin combined with alcohol can be lethal.

Another lethal combination involves taking heroin with a stimulant like cocaine, a practice called speedballing. Cocaine raises the user's heart rate in an intense rush. Then heroin, after providing its own euphoric rush, causes the heartbeat to slow down. Besides the toll it takes on the user's organs, speedballing presents a severe danger of overdose. Heroin also can be paired with fentanyl, a powerful synthetic painkiller, or other types of pain pills. Users who mix heroin with other drugs generally are seeking the high of a lifetime—with the risk of death barely an afterthought.

Quoted in Ryan Jaslow, "Cory Monteith: How Heroin and Alcohol Form Deadly Combo," CBS News, July 17, 2013. www.cbsnews.com.

inflamed gums. They may develop respiratory illnesses and weakening of the immune system. Often poor health and unsanitary living conditions make them vulnerable to pneumonia and tuberculosis. Long-term use leads to muscular weakness, backache, and arthritis. Mental problems are common, including depression, memory loss, an inability to focus, and antisocial personality disorder. Men often have trouble with sexual function, and women can have disrupted menstrual cycles. Recreational users who return to the drug after months of abstinence can face increased risk of overdose due to their bodies' failure to tolerate the drug in a strong potency. When addicts stop taking heroin for a period, whether years or even days, their tolerance is reduced. They can be killed by amounts they previously could withstand with no problem. Actor Philip Seymour Hoffman likely was blindsided by this effect.

In general, those who think they can try heroin once or twice and then stop are fooling themselves. Sam, who began using the drug at fifteen, describes the usual course: "When you first shoot up, you will most likely puke and feel repelled, but soon you'll try it again. It will cling to you like an obsessed lover. The rush of the hit and the way you'll want more, as if you were being deprived of air—that's how it will trap you."[14]

> "The rush of the hit and the way you'll want more, as if you were being deprived of air—that's how it will trap you."[14]
>
> —Sam, who began using heroin at age fifteen.

# CHAPTER 3: A Highly Addictive Substance

In 2000 Cynthia Scudo, who was then in her forties, suffered a painful hip injury. Without considering physical therapy or some other treatment option, her doctor promptly wrote her a prescription for OxyContin, a powerful pain medication. He went on to prescribe, in her words, "anything and everything"[15] to provide her with pain relief. Scudo, a slim, smartly dressed mother of eight with many grandchildren, says that by the time the doctor finally reduced her prescription, she was hooked on pain pills. With a habit of six pills a day, she would quickly run through a month's prescription. Buying OxyContin on the street in her middle-class suburb of Denver, Colorado, cost eighty dollars per pill, much more than she could afford. So to feed her habit Scudo began selling the prescription pills to pay for a cheaper form of pain relief: heroin.

## Addiction Does Not Discriminate

For Scudo, the word *heroin* conjured images of hopeless addicts under a bridge sticking a needle in their arms. Certainly she was not like that. "All my life, I heard heroin addict and thought that's the lowest of the low," she says. "[But] I stepped right into it without looking back."[16] Scudo had located painkiller dealers from among her older children's friends, and it was not too difficult to graduate to heroin purchases. For $100 she could buy 0.25 ounces (7 g) of heroin, enough to stay high for as long as three days. She did not inject the drug, having an aversion to needles, not to mention distaste for the associations of intravenous drug use. Instead, she smoked a special variety called black tar heroin. And this youngish suburban grandmother quickly became addicted to it.

Scudo generally smoked heroin late at night when her family was asleep. Using tinfoil, a straw, and a lighter, she inhaled the smoke from a pinch of the black tar heroin. She would then blow the smoke into the fan vent of her basement bathroom to prevent her kids from smelling it. Using the drug was cheap, convenient, and easy enough to rationalize with no needle involved. Yet Scudo's decade of addiction led her to take what she now sees as wildly reckless chances. Her craving simply crowded out all sensible reasoning. "I would do some crazy stuff to get drugs," she acknowledges. "Like 2 o'clock in the morning, I'm making a run to downtown Denver. Like picking up my grandkids in the car (to go to a drug deal), praying that I was not going to get busted."[17] Somehow she kept her job and even won some promotions, lying when necessary to fend off inquiries. But eventually her life began to fall apart. In her heroin-fueled haze, Scudo could not be certain how much her family knew. Her older children found excuses not to bring her grandchildren for visits. She pawned family treasures for cash. Even after her marriage broke up, she kept on stealing from her ex-husband.

> "All my life, I heard heroin addict and thought that's the lowest of the low. [But] I stepped right into it without looking back."[16]
>
> —Cynthia Scudo, a suburban grandmother and heroin addict.

Sarah Beach is another example of someone who did not fit the junkie stereotype. A successful graphic designer who lived in the San Francisco Bay Area, Beach had what most people call "it all"—a great job, a good marriage, wealth, and happiness. "Life . . . looked pretty damn sparkly from the outside," recalls Beach. "I was proud of my status as a 'respected community member,' with all the privileges that entails." But one winter she broke her knee in a bad skiing accident and had to have bone-graft surgery; over the course of recovery she became addicted first to painkillers and then, eventually, heroin. As Beach notes, "Addiction doesn't care who you are, what you have, or what you've accomplished. In under a year, I lost my marriage, my home, my baby, my dog, friends, honesty, and every scrap of my self-respect."[18]

# Why People Use Heroin

Although exact figures are unknown, heroin addicts like Cynthia Scudo and Sarah Beach probably number in the hundreds of thousands in the United States. Their condition is a recognized mental disorder called opioid use disorder. This category in the *Diagnostic and Statistical Manual of Mental Disorders* includes dependence on a range of opiates, from heroin to painkillers.

Like Scudo and Beach, many of today's heroin addicts first became hooked on pain medication, whether prescribed by a doctor or obtained on the street. Those who become addicted to heroin tend to experience more problems associated with the drug than do those addicted to other illicit substances, including marijuana, cocaine, and methamphetamine. Some research suggests that heroin's tendency to wreck lives has to do with its potent high, which is more often sought as an escape from personal problems or as a salve for emotional pain rather than for recreation. Other studies maintain that certain traits, such as

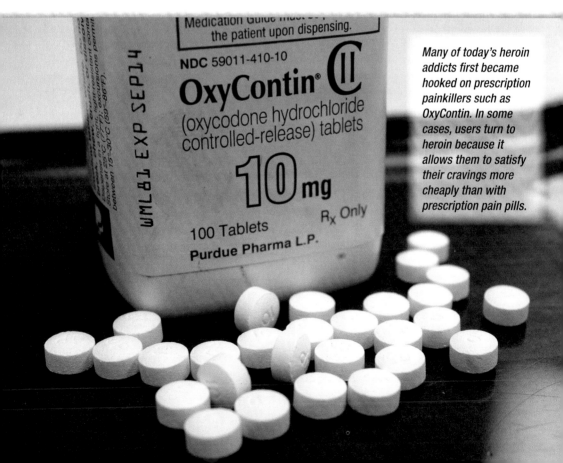

Many of today's heroin addicts first became hooked on prescription painkillers such as OxyContin. In some cases, users turn to heroin because it allows them to satisfy their cravings more cheaply than with prescription pain pills.

# Heroin-Related Crime

A silver bowl—a treasured family heirloom—disappears one day. With the garage door left open, a gas-powered hedge clipper goes missing. A handgun vanishes from its hiding place in a bedside table. Copper wires are stripped away on a neighborhood construction site. These are the sorts of thefts that make up a nonviolent-crime wave related to heroin. In southern Delaware, where heroin abuse is on the rise, addicts commit on average seventy-seven such thefts each day. Some are inflicted on friends or family members, while others take advantage of unwary strangers. The motivation for these crimes is clear: heroin addicts need quick money to feed their habit.

The crime wave is plaguing older residents in rural Delaware who associate theft with large cities and criminals on the street. Delaware police admit there is not much they can do. There are too many of these small thefts, and they do not warrant the same attention given to an armed robbery or high-dollar heist. "The vast majority of cases that we're investigating involving burglaries, when we have identified a suspect, it is directly linked to a heroin addiction," says Delaware State Police detective Josh Rowley, who handles property crime in Sussex County. "And when I say 'vast majority,' I mean almost every single one."

Quoted in James Fisher, "Heroin-Fueled Crime Wave," Delaware Online, February 14, 2015. www.delaware online.com.

recklessness or a sense of heightened stress, are key to making people more vulnerable to the drug's allure. Elizabeth Hartney, a British psychologist with a background in drug abuse and counseling, thinks the truth lies somewhere in between. As Hartney observes,

> The heroin high creates changes to thoughts, feelings and sensations, some of which are caused by the effects of the drug itself on the brain and nervous system, and some of which depend on the personal history and expectations of the person taking the drug. For this reason, one person might find the effects of heroin to be awful, while another might feel relief and pleasure from the same effects.[19]

Thus, heroin addicts turn to the drug for many reasons. Like Scudo, they may transition to the drug to replace their painkiller habit. Some pleasure seekers may drift into using it after experimenting with cocaine or crystal meth. Some may crave relief from intolerable circumstances, such as chronic depression, anxiety, job pressures, memories of past sexual abuse, or poverty. Sex workers may use it to blank out an unhappy daily reality. Young people living in dangerous neighborhoods may use it to achieve moments of calmness and safety. The homeless may simply want to escape from themselves for a while.

> "One person might find the effects of heroin to be awful, while another might feel relief and pleasure from the same effects."[19]
>
> —Elizabeth Hartney, a British psychologist with a background in drug abuse and counseling.

Whatever the reason for trying heroin, addiction does not occur with the first hit. Mainlining is rare for first-timers, as most users begin with weaker doses of the drug, snorting or sniffing it in powder form or inhaling it as smoke. This can create a misleading sense of control. "By far the biggest rumor surrounding heroin is that it's an instant addiction—you take one hit, and you're hooked," says one recovering addict. "The reality is a lot less abrupt, and a lot scarier."[20] In early stages, the user may take heroin fairly frequently with no cravings or withdrawal symptoms and may believe, mistakenly, that repeated use is no problem.

## Changes in Brain Chemistry

Regular use of heroin actually changes the brain's chemistry. Each hit of heroin floods nerve cells in the brain with dopamine, a neurotransmitter associated with feelings of pleasure. Soon the nerve cells become exhausted from repeated stimulation. The brain's response to the surge of dopamine becomes weaker. Some of the receptors in the brain apparently expire. The heroin user's pleasure from taking the drug continues to diminish even as he or she resorts to larger amounts and more frequent doses. Over time the user's system becomes accustomed to the drug's powerful effects, and it becomes harder and harder to experience the same level of pleasure as with the first few doses.

At this point users may begin injecting the drug in hopes of achieving a more intense high. As addiction takes hold, the user begins to crave more heroin within hours of the effect wearing off. Increasing amounts of the drug are needed just to feel somewhat normal. Without it, the user feels crushed, desperate, lonely, and empty. Once the brain has been conditioned to rely on heroin's euphoric rush, events of ordinary life can seem to lack point or meaning by comparison. Eventually the senses grow dull, and the ability to enjoy the ordinary pleasures of a healthy person goes away. "[Addiction] alters multiple regions in the brain," says Dr. Mary Jeanne Kreek, head of the Laboratory of the Biology of Addictive Diseases at Rockefeller University in New York City, "including those that regulate reward, memory and learning, stress responsivity, and hormonal response, as well as executive function which is involved in decision-making— simply put, when to say yes and when to say no."[21]

> "By far the biggest rumor surrounding heroin is that it's an instant addiction— you take one hit, and you're hooked. The reality is a lot less abrupt, and a lot scarier."[20]
>
> —A former heroin addict.

## Dope Sickness

Too long without a fix can lead to what addicts call dope sickness— a condition that can include restlessness, intense cramping, muscle aches, diarrhea, vomiting, and insomnia. In this state the user cares only about ensuring his or her supply. This was life for Brian, a well-to-do young addict in Harrisburg, Pennsylvania, who took to buying bundles of heroin in ten doses, the way one might buy a carton of cigarettes. To feed his habit he would blow through $280 a day. "It's insane," he admits. "That's how powerful and controlling it is. One day you're dying and the next day you're using the same thing again."[22] Ultimately, the full-blown addict can think of little else but how to score more heroin.

Behavioral conditioning only tightens the grip of addiction. All kinds of associations can trigger the addict's craving for heroin. As science writer Brian Palmer explains, "Once your brain becomes

*A Massachusetts police officer displays a bag of heroin that was confiscated as evidence during an arrest. Some addicts buy bundles of heroin in ten doses, similar to how a person might buy a carton of cigarettes.*

accustomed to the idea that eating a doughnut or having sex will provide pleasure, just seeing a doughnut or an attractive potential mate triggers the dopamine cascade into the nucleus accumbens [a small middle section of the brain]. That's part of the reason it is so difficult for recovering drug addicts to stay clean over the long term."[23] Sensory cues linked to the drug—the sight of a syringe or the voices of fellow junkies—can set off this flood of dopamine, triggering a powerful urge to take another hit.

## A Life That Revolves Around Heroin

The life of the hardened user revolves entirely around finding and taking heroin. Chance Epple, a twenty-three-year-old former user, battled heroin addiction for four years. Epple came to the drug as a cheap alternative to the painkillers he popped regularly. He recklessly went straight to the needle when he began using. Jobless and constantly high, Epple would either finagle cash from his parents or offer to perform drug buys for other addicts, skimming some of their money for his own use. Eventually he worked out an arrangement with dealers, selling heroin for them in exchange for bags. The quest for heroin took over his life. "All I did was—every day, it was a mission—waking up, trying to find more dope,"[24] says Epple.

A heroin addict wakes up in the morning feeling anything but refreshed. Aching, with watery eyes, the addict might try to get back to sleep, but then the realization hits. He or she needs heroin immediately, priority one. Nothing else matters. A young female addict from northern New Jersey describes waking up at the house of her father, who seems not to know she is back on the drug:

> I don't have to work for another 6 hours, but I have to wake up earlier than everyone else so I can sneak upstairs and steal money from my step mom's purse. This is a daily ritual at this point, especially since my habit is growing and I only get a paycheck every two weeks. I have been stealing $50-$100 a day for the last three weeks, and either she doesn't know, or doesn't want to know. . . . I take the bus down into Paterson, walk the four blocks to meet my dealer and get what I need. Since I have already started feeling sick, I make my way to Dunkin Donuts, the same one I go to every day to get high.[25]

The girl is an IV user and shoots up in the restaurant's bathroom with a needle from a needle exchange program. Her track marks are a telltale sign of a heroin addict, requiring her to wear long sleeves at home and work:

> My arms are beginning to have scar tissue so I have to switch up the vein I use each time, but I am pretty good at not missing. This is usually the point where I nod out for anywhere from 5 to 25 minutes, depending on how good the dope is. I finally shake myself awake and pack up and head back to the bus to get to work on time.[26]

# The Risk of Chipping

Some people believe they can get away with chipping, or using heroin casually as a recreational drug. In the attempt to avoid becoming addicted, they try to limit their heroin use with strict schedules, such as taking it only once a week. They tell themselves they can plan carefully and take just enough heroin to enjoy it without being saddled with a habit or suffering symptoms of withdrawal. At the first sign of addiction or dope sickness, the so-called chipper will stop cold turkey. He or she will then usually wait a while before resuming the chipping schedule.

Chippers thrive on secrecy. They take pains to hide their activities, fearing that others will assume they are addicted to heroin. Instead of going to dealers themselves, chippers may pay extra fees to use acquirers, or middlemen. After a while the chipper may get a false sense of control. The risk comes with any missteps or changes in scheduling. For example, a weekend user could make an exception for a three-day weekend and take the drug for an extra day. Back at work, the chipper may feel some ill effects and take a small amount to get back to normal. Soon the chipper is altering that careful schedule and rationalizing extra hits more and more. One day the dope sickness will necessitate missing work or some important family function. Full-blown heroin addiction is always lying in wait for even the most disciplined chipper.

At work the girl feels drowsy and cannot avoid dropping off for snatches of sleep in the bathroom or stockroom. She waits until her manager is occupied to slip into the bathroom and get high again. If the opportunity arises, she might sneak a few dollars from the cash register, oblivious to the danger of getting caught. After work she returns to Paterson for another score of heroin, six more bags. Then she rushes back to the mall just in time to be picked up by her father. She hopes he does not notice her pupils constricted to pinpoints, and she struggles to stay awake on the way home. After a few bites of dinner, she subtly scopes out exactly where her stepmother's purse will be left overnight. She is already planning the next early-morning theft. Like other heroin addicts, her life is a hectic cycle that never lets up.

# Physical Signs of Addiction

The track marks that heroin users are often at pains to hide are one of the obvious physical signs of addiction. IV users tend to accumulate needle marks, abscesses, skin infections, scars, scabs, and ugly bruises from repeated use of a syringe. Often the marks are found at the bend of the arm, but as the user wears out veins, he or she will turn elsewhere—to the back of the hands, the neck, the ankles, and sometimes between the toes. Addicts often wear sweaters or long sleeves in warm weather to conceal injection sites.

Following heroin use, the pupils of the eyes are constricted for as much as four or five hours. Persistent drowsiness is commonplace, as is yawning, slurred speech, and confusion. Another telltale sign of heroin addiction is inexplicable weight loss. Re-

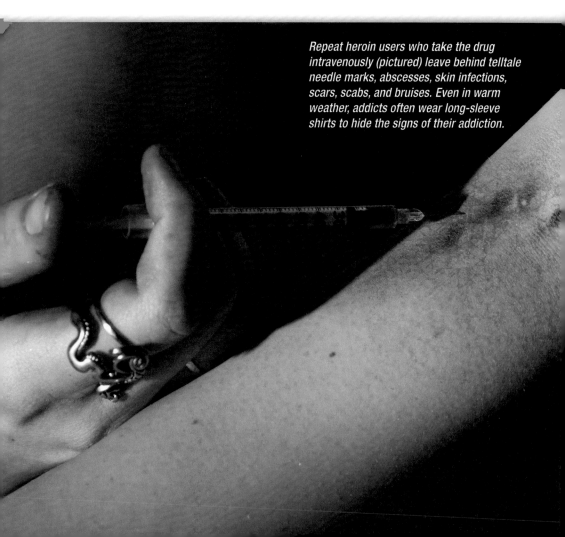

*Repeat heroin users who take the drug intravenously (pictured) leave behind telltale needle marks, abscesses, skin infections, scars, scabs, and bruises. Even in warm weather, addicts often wear long-sleeve shirts to hide the signs of their addiction.*

peated use often leaves the addict looking emaciated and in poor health. Losing weight is generally due to persistent nausea from dope sickness as well as dulled taste buds and loss of appetite. Stomach cramps and diarrhea may also contribute. Addicts trying to kick the habit may exhibit fluctuations in their weight from cycles of use and withdrawal. Also, the addict will frequently have a runny nose or dry cough. The drug's suppression of the immune system can leave the user constantly beset with low-grade infections. He or she may also suffer from cotton mouth, or dry mouth. Female addicts may experience a disrupted menstrual cycle. As one addict notes, "Listing the symptoms or even describing them cannot even begin to convey the pain and fear one experiences while going through this."[27]

# Behavioral Signs

Friends and loved ones of a person who becomes addicted to heroin may notice startling changes in behavior. For instance, an addict will often decline into a slovenly appearance and show a marked lack of interest in grooming. Long, unwashed hair; body odor; rotten teeth; and unkempt nails are common signs. Users may seem depressed or exhibit wild mood swings. They may also be secretive and angrily resist any prying questions. Often they withdraw from old friends and previous social circles in favor of new acquaintances made among dealers and other users. They may fall into slang terms or street language connected to their drug use or shady friends. They might have trouble keeping a job or begin calling in sick with increasing frequency. Hobbies or favorite leisure activities may suddenly hold no interest for the distracted addict.

The sight of paraphernalia connected to heroin use, particularly needles, should set off alarms for any concerned person. Syringes are unlikely to be left lying around, but they may be found in a wastebasket, rattling inside a soft drink can, or hidden away in drawers or medicine cabinets. IV users might also have bent spoons containing burnt residue of the drug or a cord or rubber hose to tie off the arm for injection. Those who smoke heroin may have pieces of charred tinfoil or gum wrappers in their home alongside a lighter or candle. Bongs or metal pipes are another indicator. Balloons or plastic baggies used to transport the heroin, usually emblazoned with logos or artwork, might end up carelessly tossed in the trash.

Quite often the addict learns to be manipulative to get what he or she wants or needs, whether cash, temporary shelter, or more heroin. Lying becomes habitual. Consideration for others takes a back seat to the addict's immediate cravings. "I was doing things I wouldn't dream of doing when I'm normal," says one young British heroin addict. "Stealing, staying in squats [squalid apartments], being in places I wouldn't dream of. You've got no boundaries, which is wrong. And you lose all of your emotions, you know. You don't feel guilty, it's just, 'Me, me, me, I want that, I need that,' and you don't think of others, what it does to others."[28] Deborah Pringle, director of a substance abuse treatment center, agrees that heroin is among many drugs that cause people to break the trust of their loved ones, sometimes over and over. "[Addicts] are not remorseful when they're high," Pringle notes. "But when they come off their high, it's, 'Oh, I can't believe I stooped this low, to steal from my grandma.'"[29]

> "I was doing things I wouldn't dream of doing when I'm normal. . . . You don't feel guilty, it's just, 'Me, me, me, I want that, I need that,' and you don't think of others, what it does to others."[28]
>
> —A young British heroin addict.

The lure of euphoria and the endless chase after a diminishing pleasure give heroin its psychological hold over the addict. The drug's disruption of the brain's chemistry helps to snare the addict physically as well. Breaking heroin's grip on today's users—many of whom are young adults who originally got hooked on painkillers—and preventing the creation of future addicts represents a huge challenge in the years ahead.

# CHAPTER 4: The Challenges of Treatment and Recovery

**W**hen Angela Cicchino talks to heroin addicts about hitting rock bottom, she speaks from experience. In 2011 she was hunkered down in an abandoned house in Toms River, New Jersey. The house lacked electricity and running water, and a shower was a rare luxury, but that was the least of Cicchino's concerns. All she could think about was how to score her next fix of heroin. Dying seemed preferable to facing the world without the drug. Only when she was arrested for possession and hauled off to jail did her life begin to change. A judge ordered that she enter a treatment program for opiate addiction, which provided a support network that no doubt saved her life. Knowing the importance of feeling one is not alone, she is using her experience to help other heroin addicts get the support they need.

## Recovery Specialist

Cicchino works as a recovery specialist in a two-year pilot effort called the New Jersey Opioid Overdose Recovery Program. The program, run by the health care network Barnabas Health, targets users who have overdosed on heroin or painkillers and have been revived with naloxone, the medication that reverses the effects of opiate overdose. After recovery at Community Medical Center in Toms River or some other facility, patients are urged to accept professional treatment. The key is that those steering users into treatment are recovering addicts themselves who know how crucial it is to get help. As a recovering addict, Cicchino can make the case to users in ways that ring true and are especially persuasive. "They don't trust anyone," she says.

They're going through withdrawal, they're angry. They don't want to talk. . . . We come in and let them know who we are, what we've been through and there's that connection. I've had some patients that want to go right away and I've had some that curse me off. You've got to let them know you have compassion and there is hope. We don't give up on them whether they've given up on themselves or not.[30]

The New Jersey program and similar ones in other states have impressed experts in heroin treatment and withdrawal therapy. The numbers tell the story. A previous program initiated by Barnabas Health managed to convince only 2 out of 150 naloxone patients to undergo detoxification—ridding the body of dangerous toxins from drug abuse—and neither of those patients lasted more than a couple of days. By contrast, between January and March 2016 recovery specialists like Cicchino persuaded 35 of 57 overdose victims to enter detox or long-term treatment, a success rate of more than 60 percent.

After the patients are in treatment, the recovery coaches then provide them with at least eight weeks of non-clinical advice and support. The value of recovering addicts making their own urgent case for treatment is hard to deny. New Jersey governor Chris Christie has proposed funding of $1.7 million for the program. As Christie observes, "From people who know what it is to have an addiction, the advice and counseling and help that comes from people who have been exactly where these folks are—there's no way to substitute that."[31]

> "You've got to let them know you have compassion and there is hope. We don't give up on them whether they've given up on themselves or not."[30]
>
> —Angela Cicchino, a recovering addict and now a recovery specialist in the New Jersey Opioid Overdose Recovery Program.

## A Gradual Process

For heroin addicts like those in Angela Cicchino's program, the decision to seek help is momentous—and potentially lifesaving. Heroin is one of the world's most addictive substances, and overcoming heroin addiction requires enormous commitment and effort on the part of the patient. Above all, the heroin addict should never try to detox from the drug alone, even though the temptation to try may be great. The user may have difficulty interacting with strangers, harbor suspicions about anyone offering help, or seek to avoid the embarrassment of publicly admitting he or she has a problem.

Some websites offer advice on conducting a home heroin detox, but such suggestions are misguided and actually lead the addict in the wrong direction. Despite their pretense of no-nonsense honesty, these self-styled experts often play down the serious dangers of withdrawal, as if detoxification from heroin can be achieved in a few days or a long weekend. According to Marc Myer, a physician who treats opioid addiction and a recovering addict himself, "Sometimes patients will ask, 'Doc, when am I going to feel better?' And I sometimes don't want to tell them that it's going to be awhile. It's hard to ride that line between being realistic and not removing hope."[32]

In reality, detoxing at home or without the supervision of a licensed doctor with experience in treating heroin dependence and withdrawal is unsafe and almost certain to fail. Successful

*A doctor talks with her patient. Those who stand the best chance of overcoming heroin addiction seek out help from trained addiction counselors and other medical professionals.*

# An Underused Antiaddiction Drug

At the Tom Waddell Urban Health Clinic in San Francisco, Dr. Kelly Eagen sees firsthand the wreckage caused by heroin abuse. Her patients often are homeless and suffer from hideous withdrawal symptoms, including a desperate craving for drugs. Yet Eagen has a powerful tool at her disposal to help these patients get control of their lives and begin to live without opiates. The tool is the antiaddiction medicine buprenorphine, which blocks heroin's effect on the brain's opiate receptors. Programs like Eagen's that employ this drug offer heroin addicts a far better chance of recovery than does reliance on counseling and 12-step programs. Yet use of buprenorphine remains limited mostly to big-city clinics.

The problem is a federal law that restricts the number of US doctors authorized to prescribe buprenorphine to fewer than thirty-two thousand nationwide. This number is dwarfed by the almost nine hundred thousand who can prescribe pain pills. Because of the restrictions, clinics in small towns and rural areas—where nurse practitioners and physician assistants may be the only care providers for addicts—do not generally have access to this valuable treatment option. Also, many qualified doctors seem reluctant to prescribe the drug without more training on how to use it. Other physicians, however, believe the federal restrictions go too far and are lobbying for more use of buprenorphrine. "We doctors are the ones who caused this epidemic by overprescribing pain medications," says Kelly Pfeifer, a physician with the California HealthCare Foundation. "We need to get more involved in fixing it."

Quoted in *Huffington Post*, "Few Doctors Are Willing, Able to Prescribe Powerful Anti-Addiction Drugs," January 15, 2016. www.huffingtonpost.com.

withdrawal must be accomplished in a gradual process, often with the aid of bridge narcotics that help reduce symptoms and wean the addict off heroin. Abrupt withdrawal—stopping all at once, or going "cold turkey"—results in severe, excruciating, and potentially dangerous symptoms.

In addition, no detox program has a chance of working without professional counseling. If the addict is not guided to change his or her behavior and outlook, and taught how to live life without heroin, that person will simply slide back into using at the first opportunity. Heroin addiction must be approached as the deadly condition it is. As such, successful treatment calls for the expertise of trained medical professionals and counselors. People like Cicchino and her recovery coaches, with their firsthand knowledge of what it takes to break away from heroin, can also help addicts cope with the arduous road ahead of them.

## The Symptoms of Withdrawal

Heroin withdrawal affects those who have taken the drug consistently enough to develop a tolerance. These users are physically and psychologically addicted. Physically their brain cells have adjusted over time to help them survive the influx of heroin and remain conscious. Damaged brain cells take time to repair, to go from needing heroin to not needing it, and to regain their sensitivity to dopamine. As the cells slowly reverse the damage, they often do not function properly. The impaired cells may leave the recovering heroin addict barely able to enjoy even ordinary pleasures and thus more prone to depression.

Heroin addicts begin to experience withdrawal each time the drug's effects wear off, about six to twelve hours after the previous dose. It is this recurrence of what addicts call dope sickness—feeling lousy and rundown, with a dry mouth, watery eyes, and aching muscles—that sends them in search of a fix in order to feel what passes for normal again. When an addict first stops using heroin entirely, withdrawal becomes acute. With no medication, the symptoms of withdrawal grow more and more intense, usually reaching their most severe level about two to three days after the last hit. In general, the more often a person has taken the drug, the more difficult the experience of withdrawal will be.

Addicts describe the physical symptoms of withdrawal from heroin as feeling much like a horrible case of the flu—or the super flu, as some have called it. Symptoms include bone and joint pains, stomach cramps, sweating, fever and chills, tremors and muscle spasms, nausea, vomiting, diarrhea, and overall restlessness. These symptoms are rarely life threatening, but they can be dangerous for addicts who are already weakened and in poor health.

The psychological effects that go along with withdrawal symptoms can make them seem almost impossible to endure. The addict is seized with an overpowering desire for heroin, like water for a person dying of thirst. This craving, its strength and persistence, looms as the most difficult part of heroin withdrawal for many sufferers. Ian McLoone, an expert in behavioral health counseling, explains:

> In the moment, when you are experiencing the first few stages of withdrawal, even though you know the worst that's going to happen is that you will feel like you have the flu, there's a psychological piece that is so terrifying and so disconcerting. You know that there's a cure, and you know that it's out there, and that's why people will go to such lengths to quell those withdrawal symptoms. Even though it's ridiculous and it's weak and it's pitiful, in the moment, it really seems like it's the worst thing that can ever possibly happen. Isn't that weird?"[33]

## Overcoming the Obstacles to Recovery

It is at the point when withdrawal symptoms are most severe that the risk of relapse on heroin is greatest. The addict will consider using the drug again just to relieve the nightmarish distress and discomfort of withdrawal. He or she might see such a relapse as a failure of willpower. The idea of quitting for good may seem absurd when the addict has so much trouble lasting even a few days without the drug. For the hard-core addict, ending the cycle of addiction, withdrawal, and relapse and moving toward recovery is all but impossible without outside help. Inpatient treatment and support by medical professionals provides the only viable method of escaping the tenacious grip of heroin.

Getting treatment for heroin abuse helps the addict overcome the main obstacles to recovery. First, a treatment program will address the terrible withdrawal symptoms that eat away at an addict's resolve to change his or her behavior. If a patient's

*The risk of relapse is greatest when withdrawal symptoms are most severe. Medication can help suppress some of the symptoms, making it less likely that the addict will sabotage his or her own recovery by starting up use again.*

symptoms are suppressed with medication, the person is less likely to sabotage the quest for recovery by falling back on heroin use.

Medical personnel can help a patient understand that recovery is not solely a question of willpower. While strong will plays a role, the patient's brain must actually be reprogrammed—rewired almost—to overcome heroin addiction. The patient must also recognize that kicking the habit is a long-term process. A month in a rehab center represents only the first step. To root out the addiction, the patient must steel himself or herself for years of follow-up therapy and inevitable setbacks. "It never stops," admits Ethan Romeo, who has spent years in and out of treatment programs in Massachusetts. "Addiction never stops, and I will live with this for the rest of my life, but there are ways to maintain control."[34]

Perhaps most important, treatment can instill a realistic attitude about relapse. Backsliding into heroin use should be viewed not as a discouraging failure but instead as a setback that is not uncommon on the road to recovery. After all, the addict's brain is divided in a constant battle. Part of it realizes the awful consequences of using heroin, but another part is burning to take the drug again *right now*.

Soon after beginning treatment, the dangers of relapse are greatest. Relapse can be triggered by stress, frustration, depression, fear, and anxiety. The addict may crave heroin as a way to cope with daily reality. Another trigger for relapse is returning to places where the addict's heroin use occurred or seeing people connected with the drug habit. Recovering addicts sometimes romanticize their heroin use and convince themselves that using was pleasurable and exciting. With clinical support and understanding, the patient can more easily bounce back from a relapse. Medical personnel, having seen it all before, can offer realistic guidance about what to expect along the way. Sadly, relapse can occur even after years of being clean.

> "Addiction never stops, and I will live with this for the rest of my life, but there are ways to maintain control."[34]
>
> —Ethan Romeo, an addict in Ware, Massachusetts.

## Replacement Therapies

Once a patient is placed in a rehab center, doctors can use special drugs to help that person make it through withdrawal. The type of medications used depends on the severity of the addict's condition and his or her commitment to kicking the habit. Doctors can treat milder cases of heroin addiction with naltrexone, a drug that blocks the effect of any heroin in the person's system. The patient can then be given clonidine, which relieves many of the symptoms of withdrawal. The combination of naltrexone and clonidine has proven very effective for heroin addicts whose cravings for the drug are less intense and can be controlled with counseling.

# An Addict Describes Her Withdrawal from Heroin

Sarah Beach has known the depths of heroin withdrawal and the surprise of a possible cure by taking Suboxone. Here she describes her agony and her feelings of hope:

> The closest I've ever come to describing [withdrawal] to a friend is: You know when you're underwater, and you need to come up for a breath? And it's taking too long to get to the surface? That feeling, of having no oxygen left, your whole body feeling like fire, salty and aching with the desperate need to breathe? That's it, only not exactly, because it's worse.

Finally Beach checked in to a detox clinic, where she was given the drug Suboxone to relieve her withdrawal symptoms:

> I had just drawn in another ragged breath for another moan of agony, when it all . . . suddenly . . . STOPPED. What?! I sat up. My body was still and calm. The feeling of bugs crawling in and out of my skin vanished. My stomach settled and my head stopped whirling. The worst thing—the indescribable feeling of whole-body horror—was simply gone. . . . The sunlight felt amazing on my face. Tears came to my eyes, but I laughed.

Sarah Beach, "It Happened to Me: I Went Through the Hell of Heroin Withdrawal and Came Out the Other Side," xoJane, October 30, 2013. www.xojane.com.

More severe cases call for replacement therapies to assist the body in adjusting to lack of heroin. The drug buprenorphine—marketed under the brand name Suboxone—is a prescription painkiller that works on the same brain receptors as heroin but without the euphoric effect or associated high. It can eliminate the worst effects of withdrawal and enable the recovering addict to feel close to normal. If an even stronger medication is needed, doctors can provide methadone. This drug is very similar to heroin but lasts even longer in the user's system. Methadone provides more effective relief from withdrawal symptoms. A heroin addict who displays willingness to get clean may be steered to a program that provides regular doses of methadone as a replacement for heroin. The idea is to help the addict avoid contact with street sellers of heroin and other drugs, with an eye toward ending his or her drug use entirely.

> "If I have a medication that can reduce those urges [for heroin] and allow a person to participate in life normally, what's wrong with that?"[35]
>
> —Dr. David Suetholz, coroner in Kenton County, Kentucky.

Not everyone supports the use of replacement therapies. Some critics point to the fact that Suboxone and methadone are themselves addictive drugs. They feel that replacement therapy essentially just trades out one drug for another, without changing the addict's behavior. But others see it as humane medical treatment. "We're not contributing to the addiction," says Dr. David Suetholz, coroner in Kenton County, Kentucky. "What we're giving people is a light at the end of the tunnel. If I have urges once I leave a treatment program, these urges could potentially kill me. So, if I have a medication that can reduce those urges and allow a person to participate in life normally, what's wrong with that?"[35]

# Psychotherapy and Cognitive Behavioral Therapy

After the physical symptoms of withdrawal have been addressed, the next stage of treatment focuses on the psychological factors that led the addict to heroin. One method is called cognitive behavioral therapy (CBT). Introduced in the 1960s, CBT originally was developed to treat depression. However, it has been found effective in treating a variety of conditions, including drug addiction, alcoholism, and eating disorders. CBT focuses on the heroin addict's dysfunctional thinking patterns—negative thoughts that repeatedly enter the person's mind. In individual counseling sessions, a therapist can help the recovering user identify those automatic thoughts that feed the cycle of addictive behavior. For example, the addict might be helped to recognize that he often thinks, "Why shouldn't

I shoot up heroin? I'm a worthless person anyway." The therapist might then teach him to change that thought to "I deserve a healthier life. I'm a worthwhile person after all."

Another psychological approach is contingency management. This encourages the heroin addict to refrain from using by giving him or her positive reinforcement when treatment goals are met. Should the addict fall short of goals or have a relapse, he or she receives some sort of punishment. For example, meeting goals might allow the addict to receive vouchers for merchandise, but relapse would result in withholding vouchers or delivering a negative report to the addict's parole officer. Besides CBT and

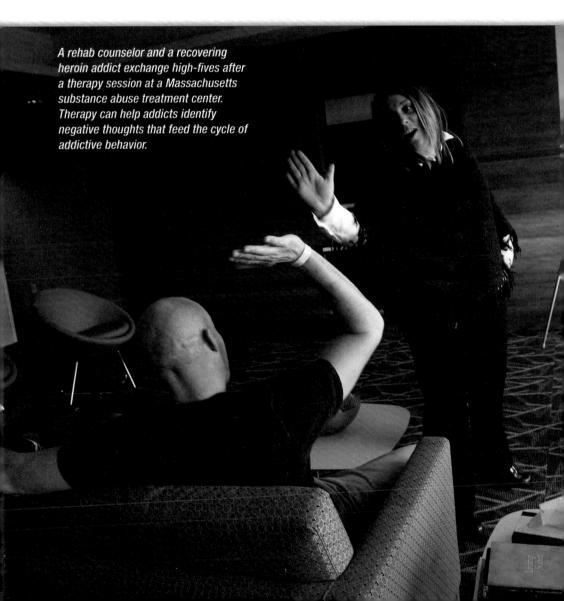

A rehab counselor and a recovering heroin addict exchange high-fives after a therapy session at a Massachusetts substance abuse treatment center. Therapy can help addicts identify negative thoughts that feed the cycle of addictive behavior.

contingency management, the heroin addict may enter a traditional 12-step program like Narcotics Anonymous. In these types of programs, the addict shares stories and receives support from others with similar experiences.

Debate continues about the best way to treat heroin addiction. Increasingly, medical experts advise the use of antiaddiction medications to break the drug's grip on the brain. Medication combined with long-term psychological counseling and support seem to present the most effective approach. Nearly everyone agrees that relying on the addict's willpower alone to quit the drug offers little chance of success.

# CHAPTER 5: Preventing Heroin Abuse

The commercial begins with the sound of a ukulele playing a lilting tune. A teenager sits on his rumpled bed in a drowsy haze. One nostril shows traces of white powder. Next to him is a little plastic bag of pills. He cannot keep his eyes open, and finally he passes out and falls backward. His mother walks into his room to discover him lying motionless on his bed. She tries to wake him, spots the plastic bag, and then holds him and begins to sob. To the bouncy musical accompaniment, a female voice sings, "That's how, how you OD'd on heroin."[36]

During the 2015 Super Bowl, this controversial ad played locally in St. Louis. The ad's sponsor, the National Council on Alcoholism & Drug Abuse (NCADA), targeted St. Louis because of the epidemic there of heroin and painkiller abuse. Those who actually saw the ad disagreed about its effect, some labeling it creepy and others courageous. In explaining the rationale for the ad, NCADA director Howard Weissman observed that more than twenty-three hundred young people in the region had lost their lives to heroin since 2007. "The stark contrast in tone between the upsetting images and the almost lighthearted music is an intentional choice that reflects the stark contrasts of these real-life situations," explains NCADA. "In using the tools of drama to convey this crucial truth in a 60-second spot, we created a parallel disconnection between the visual story we see on screen and the musical story we hear. It is disturbing. It is jarring. It is painful to watch. And we must pay attention to it."[37]

## Awakening to the Problem

Ads like that 2015 Super Bowl spot demonstrate how the nation is awakening to the growing problem of heroin abuse. Of course, the problem is not exactly new. As far back as November 1997 the National Institutes of Health (NIH) organized a panel of experts to delve into the issue of heroin addiction and treatment. The panel, made up of physicians, treatment providers, and drug-policy experts, acknowledged that heroin abuse had become an urgent public health issue.

The panel declared that heroin and other opiate drug addictions are diseases of the brain, not failures of will or character, and that they can be treated like other medical problems. It stressed the value of drugs like methadone and buprenorphine in treating heroin addicts and suggested lowering legal barriers to using these drugs in treatment. It also suggested more use of cognitive behavioral therapy and other counseling therapies that research had found effective. These therapies, combined with methadone maintenance programs, could lead to more successful outcomes. The NIH conference marked the first steps in establishing a national policy on preventing heroin abuse and treating those who become addicted to the drug and other opiates. Its recommendations, with a few adjustments, remain valid to this day.

More recently, in March 2016, the Obama administration announced efforts to stem the heroin epidemic in America. One focus was to make it easier for doctors to prescribe antiaddiction drugs for heroin treatment—a step first proposed in 1997. The White House increased the number of patients for which a doctor can prescribe buprenorphine from one hundred to two hundred and also supported state and local efforts to double the number of physicians nationwide who are qualified to prescribe the drug. Among other initiatives in the White House plan were more funds for naloxone, the drug that can reverse heroin overdose; funds for the Department of Justice (DOJ) to police and investigate heroin distribution; and guidance from the Department of Health and Human Services to set up needle exchange programs in areas hardest hit by the epidemic.

The White House is encouraged that thirty-five states and the District of Columbia have passed so-called Good Samaritan laws, which support and protect those who make good-faith efforts to help heroin abusers and overdose victims. One benefit is increas-

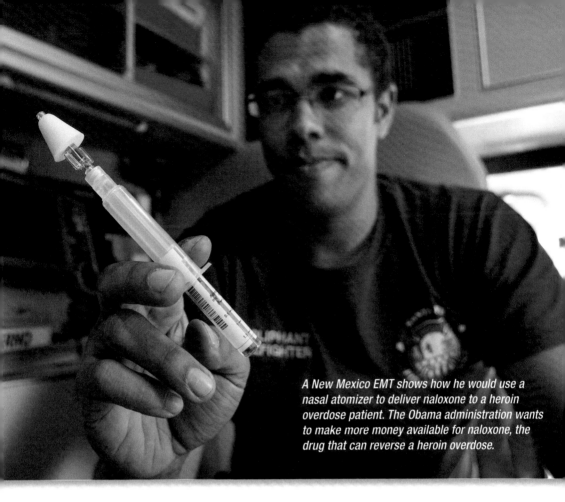

A New Mexico EMT shows how he would use a nasal atomizer to deliver naloxone to a heroin overdose patient. The Obama administration wants to make more money available for naloxone, the drug that can reverse a heroin overdose.

ing access to naloxone. "Often family and friends are in the best position to administer this lifesaving drug to their loved ones who overdose because they are able to react more quickly," notes the National Conference of State Legislatures. "Providing medication to anyone other than the at-risk drug user . . . was previously prohibited and laws required a doctor-patient relationship to be established prior to direct prescription."[38]

Before passage of Good Samaritan laws, even medical professionals were often reluctant to prescribe naloxone because of fears of criminal or professional liability. The laws also protect police officers and other nonmedical personnel from liability when administering naloxone to a person suffering from heroin or opioid-related overdose. For a person who calls 911 to report a heroin overdose, Good Samaritan laws can provide legal immunity from possession charges or parole violations related to the

# Following Seattle's LEAD

Turina James is a familiar sight on the streets of Belltown, a neighborhood of Seattle, Washington. Her hand is wrapped from an old injury suffered while she was shooting heroin. She first tried heroin when she was seventeen, shortly after her baby son died. James has often lived on the streets, sometimes sleeping in a parking garage. When Seattle police arrested her on a possession charge, they gave her a novel choice. Instead of going to jail, she could join a new program called LEAD, which would provide a counselor to help get her life in order. James promptly agreed.

LEAD, which stands for Law Enforcement Assisted Diversion, is an innovative program that helps heroin addicts like James embark on a path to recovery. LEAD officers are specially trained to patrol neighborhoods like Belltown and keep an eye out for repeat drug offenders and individuals at risk. The officers seek to break the cycle of repeat arrests related to narcotics. Those who join LEAD can stay in the program even if they continue to use drugs or are arrested for another crime. Najja Morris, the counselor assigned to James, found her a small hotel room and checks up on her regularly. Morris has become a trusted friend, striving to keep James away from the dealers who constantly appear on the street corners in Belltown. "We work for [users in need] and show up for them," says Morris, "and eventually they decide they're going to work and show up for themselves."

Quoted in Adam Desiderio, Jessica Puckett, and Alexa Valiente, "Why a Seattle Police Program Wants to Keep Low-Level Drug Offenders Out of Jail," ABC News, October 7, 2015. http://abcnews.go.com.

person's own heroin use. "My clients (or families on their behalf) don't want to be convicted felons," says Daniel Schubert, a Kentucky attorney who has represented heroin abusers. "They don't want prison sentences. They don't want criminal arrests. If that is where they believe a 911 call will lead, then they won't call."[39]

## Getting Help Through Law Enforcement

New thinking about heroin treatment is making inroads at every level of government in the United States. Drug policy experts consider Good Samaritan laws, buprenorphine plans, and needle exchange programs to be more sensible and humane than policies of the past. Now, some localities are changing the way police approach the war on heroin. No longer do officers focus solely on arresting addicts as punishment for their drug habit. The feeling is that jail cannot reverse their addiction. Instead, addicts are encouraged to turn themselves in at the police station and voluntarily take the first step on the road to recovery.

An example of such a program comes from Gloucester, Massachusetts. Picture the following scene: A young woman with a black eye shows up at the local precinct one evening battling a bad case of withdrawal sickness. She confesses to having a heroin habit and also describes being abused by her boyfriend. She has been living on the street for three days, injecting heroin. A relative picked her up and delivered her to the police station.

After a few questions, officers usher the woman into a holding cell where she can sleep overnight. However, she is not under arrest. Under a new policy regarding heroin and opioid addicts, the woman is turned over to volunteers and trained clinicians who will connect her with a detox center for immediate treatment. "It was better than the alternative," she says. "I just knew if I was let go, I'd just go out and use."[40] Addicts also are urged to surrender their heroin, painkillers, and any drug-taking paraphernalia to the police with no penalty. Money for treatment comes from public and private insurance, federal grants, and cash confiscated from dealers in drug busts.

> "My clients (or families on their behalf) don't want to be convicted felons. . . . If that is where they believe a 911 call will lead, then they won't call."[39]
>
> —Daniel Schubert, a Kentucky attorney who has represented heroin abusers.

In the program's first two months, more than a hundred addicts sought help from the police and ended up in treatment facilities. All told, the effort cost the Gloucester police department about $5,000. However, the program is not without its critics. A prosecutor in Gloucester cautions that police assurances about not charging addicts with a crime may lack legal authority. Officials at treatment centers worry that the program might flood the system with new patients, affecting their ability to provide adequate care. Nonetheless, the initiative is winning support. Impressed by early results, residents in Gloucester have organized a nonprofit group to support the program and share its ideas with other communities. Inspired by Gloucester's success, some cities, such as Dixon, Illinois, are already adapting the new approach to help heroin addicts. "Traditionally, law enforcement has tried to arrest their way out of the problem," says Dixon police chief Dan Langloss. "That just doesn't work."[41]

## Treatment, Not Prison

Other states are beginning to focus their antiopioid efforts on getting help for addicts instead of throwing them in prison. The shift reflects national polls that show Americans favor treatment for drug users over prison terms by a margin of two to one.

Vermont, one of several northeastern states facing a crisis due to a flood of cheap heroin, is turning to a comprehensive approach that reflects these new attitudes. The state now sends nonviolent drug offenders to treatment centers rather than court. They proceed first to one of the central recovery clinics, or hubs, which are part of an interconnected, state-supported system that has earned praise as one of the nation's finest. Once they are weaned off of heroin or pain medication, patients then can seek further treatment with a family physician or therapist. As another incentive, Vermont passed a law to shield users who need emergency care for an overdose from being prosecuted for selling or possessing drugs. Vermont was also the first state to allow over-the-counter sales of naloxone, the drug that can reverse opioid overdose. This move enables friends, family members, or even fellow junkies to act as first responders should an episode of heroin use take a sinister turn.

> "Traditionally, law enforcement has tried to arrest their way out of the problem [of heroin abuse]. That just doesn't work."[41]
>
> —Dan Langloss, police chief in Dixon, Illinois.

For Vermont governor Peter Shumlin, the new approach is more rational than the aggressive—and mostly ineffective—war on drugs that for decades targeted users as criminals. Shumlin

In 2016 Governor Peter Shumlin of Vermont testifies before a Senate committee about the impact of heroin addiction on his state. Vermont has changed the way it deals with heroin addiction.

has brought the heroin issue to the forefront of Vermont politics and has tried to replace the stigma attached to addiction with a more understanding attitude. "We've changed the conversation," Shumlin says about his state's efforts. "This isn't an issue to be ashamed about any more than you should be ashamed of getting cancer or kidney disease."[42]

While the scale of Vermont's antiopioid program is impressive, with funding for treatment nearly tripling in 2015, Shumlin knows that constraints on budget and medical personnel could limit some of its potential. He admitted as much in a February 2016 White House meeting with President Obama, who shares his enthusiasm for the new approach. "As you build out treatment, and particularly in rural America, we can't get enough [doctors] who are able to meet the demand of our waiting lists,"[43] Shumlin told the president. Alarmingly, despite the new programs and the more thoughtful approach, heroin use and heroin-related deaths continue to rise in Vermont.

# High School Guardians Fight Heroin

Butler County, in southwestern Ohio, has an enormous heroin problem. To understand the roots of the problem, county prosecutor Mike Gmoser reached out to young heroin addicts in the area. Gmoser started a hotline and placed alerts in the media, asking heroin addicts to speak with him confidentially about how they got hooked on the drug. Dozens responded with harrowing stories. Many admitted they started using heroin after taking prescription painkillers to treat an injury or to relieve anxiety from memories of childhood abuse. "They said nobody explained to us that this would take us, shake us and kill us," says Gmoser.

This insight led Gmoser to start the Guardians program. The idea is based on efforts to discourage drunk driving and alcohol abuse. Older students engage in peer counseling, acting as guardians to counsel students one year below them about the deadly grip of heroin and other opioid drugs. During the school year each guardian meets four times with his or her assigned student. The pairs are encouraged to discuss pressures to try heroin or other drugs as well as issues at home and emotional concerns. Recovering addicts will also speak at specially arranged school assemblies, delivering raw, unfiltered accounts of heroin addiction. Susan Cross Lipnickey, head of the Butler County Opiate Abuse Task Force, is cautiously optimistic about the program's potential. "I think education is important. [But] not everything works for everybody," she says. "It's a complex problem and we're all looking for a silver bullet."

Quoted in Sheila McLaughlin, "Anti-Heroin Plan: High School 'Guardians,'" Cincinnati.com, August 15, 2014. www.cincinnati.com.

## A White, Middle-Class Problem

The push toward decriminalizing heroin use—treating it less like a crime and more like an affliction—strikes some observers as being connected to questions of race and class. They note that attitudes are changing now that the heroin problem affects so many white suburbanites. According to *New York Times* reporter Katharine Q. Seelye,

> When the nation's long-running war against drugs was defined by the crack epidemic and based in poor, pre-

dominantly black urban areas, the public response was defined by zero tolerance and stiff prison sentences. But today's heroin crisis is different. While heroin use has climbed among all demographic groups, it has skyrocketed among whites. . . . And the growing army of families of those lost to heroin—many of them in the suburbs and small towns—are now using their influence, anger and grief to cushion the country's approach to drugs, from altering the language around addiction to prodding government to treat it not as a crime, but as a disease.[44]

Parents of young, white, middle-class heroin addicts have been effective in urging legislatures and law enforcement officials to stress compassion and treatment in dealing with drug offenders. In 2015 the DOJ announced the release of six thousand inmates held on drug charges due to retroactive changes in sentencing guidelines. In an interview that aired on PBS's *Frontline*, former attorney general Eric Holder agreed that many of the new, more lenient public health responses to heroin addiction have to do with the fact that it is now young whites who are getting hooked. Even White House advocates for change in drug policy deliberately chose the word *epidemic* in referring to the heroin problem to emphasize the connection to the idea of disease. It was a usage the news media was quick to adopt.

# A Change in the Global War on Heroin

New thinking also pervades the US approach to the global war on the heroin trade. Leaders around the world now agree that longtime law enforcement efforts to hobble heroin production and use were mostly a waste of time and money. "A war that has been fought for more than 40 years has not been won," says President Juan Manuel Santos of Colombia, a nation that remains a large producer of heroin and a hub of the international drug trade. "When you do something for 40 years and it doesn't work, you need to change it."[45]

The United States has acknowledged the spotty success of the drug wars. As it focuses more on treating heroin and other

Joaquin "El Chapo" Guzman, head of the Sinaloa drug cartel in Mexico, is arrested in 2014. The long-running war on drugs has not eliminated the drug trade and might even have increased power and profits for the drug cartels.

drugs as a public health problem, the Obama administration seeks ways to slow heroin trafficking in Mexico, Colombia, and Guatemala without resorting to violent confrontations with the cartels. Besides, some experts argue that attacking the Mexican cartels actually helps them. When the cost of transporting heroin rises because of the danger involved, the cartels are able to charge more, thus increasing profits. Certainly the Mexican cartels have greatly increased opium production and have concentrated their operations on heroin trafficking in the United States in recent years. As their product makes its way to suburbs and small towns in middle America, drug lords—such as the notorious Joaquin "El Chapo" Guzman, head of the Sinaloa drug cartel—continue to amass wealth and power. Even more troubling, corrupt Mexican law officers often are giving the cartels a helping hand.

Another place where US antiheroin policy has hit a roadblock is Afghanistan, the world's largest producer of opium poppies. For more than a decade, the United States has tried to wipe out the opium economy in that nation. The idea has been that banning the production of poppies and opium would end the market for these products. This in turn would aid the war on terror by cutting off income from the Taliban, a group of violent religious extremists that has plagued the Afghan people.

The actual result, however, was to push the opium trade underground, creating a thriving black market. Smaller producers, harassed by fines and jail time doled out by US-backed local officials, mostly left the field to larger groups, particularly the Taliban. Ordinary Afghanis, desperately needing jobs, have joined the Taliban's criminal enterprise as the only game in town. In the end, not only is the heroin trade thriving like never before, but the Taliban holds more power than when US forces first arrived. Afghanis who might have been allies in the war on terror instead view Americans with suspicion. And the illegal heroin trade helps spread more corruption throughout the Afghan government. "Not only have US policies to eliminate drugs in Afghanistan failed," says Abigail Hall, an assistant professor of economics at the University of Tampa in Florida, "but they have worked to undermine some of its broader goals in the region."[46]

> "Not only have US policies to eliminate drugs in Afghanistan failed, but they have worked to undermine some of its broader goals in the region."[46]
>
> —Abigail Hall, an assistant professor of economics at the University of Tampa.

# Unintended Consequences

Where heroin is involved, the law of unintended consequences seems to rule—from Afghanistan to the streets of sleepy towns and suburbs in the United States. Attempts to stem a painkiller epidemic helped lead to a heroin epidemic. Laws intended to crack down on drug use discouraged people from helping an overdose victim. Drug abuse experts hope that more humane policies of replacement therapy and decriminalization will help more heroin addicts to achieve a lasting recovery. As for any new policies, however, the ultimate consequences are impossible to predict.

# SOURCE NOTES

## Chapter 1: A Drug on the Rise—Again

1. Quoted in Sara Nathan et al., "'If I Don't Stop I Know I'm Going to Die': How Tragic Philip Seymour Hoffman Predicted His Fate Weeks Before Fatal Heroin Overdose," *Daily Mail*, February 3, 2014. www.dailymail.co.uk.
2. Quoted in James Nye, "Former Bowie Saxophonist Blamed for Selling Philip Seymour Hoffman Heroin Claims He Is Being Made a Scapegoat for the Actor's Death," *Daily Mail*, April 13, 2014. www.dailymail.co.uk.
3. Quoted in Daniel A. Medina, Victor Limjoco, and Kate Snow, "'Our Families Are Dying': New Hampshire's Heroin Crisis," NBC News, February 3, 2016. www.nbcnews.com.
4. Quoted in Kelsey Dallas and Sandy Balazic, "How Heroin Made Its Way to the Suburbs," *Las Vegas Review-Journal*, February 19, 2015. www.reviewjournal.com.
5. Todd C. Frankel, "Following Heroin's Path from Mexico to the Midwest," *Washington Post*, September 24, 2015. www.washingtonpost.com.

## Chapter 2: The Effects of Heroin Abuse

6. Quoted in Sam Bonacci, "Ethan's Story, Part 2: 'From the Very First Time I Shot Heroin I Immediately Fell in Love,'" MassLive, April 9, 2014. www.masslive.com.
7. Quoted in David Allegretti, "Former Users Describe the First Time They Tried Heroin," *Vice*, November 6, 2015. www.vice.com.
8. Quoted in Jen Christensen, "How Heroin Kills You," CNN, August 29, 2014. www.cnn.com.
9. Quoted in Bonacci, "Ethan's Story, Part 2."
10. Meg Thomas, "Drug Misuse—the Risks of Intravenous Drug Use," *GP*, November 19, 2009. www.gponline.com.

11. Quoted in TheBodyPRO.com, "Sniffing, Snorting Drugs May Raise Hepatitis C Risk," July 9, 2003. www.thebodypro.com.

12. Quoted in *Irish Examiner*, "Special Report Day 1: The Real Story Behind Heroin Use," November 18, 2013. www.irish examiner.com.

13. Sarah Beach, "It Happened to Me: I Went Through the Hell of Heroin Withdrawal and Came Out the Other Side," xoJane .com, October 30, 2013. www.xojane.com.

14. Quoted in Foundation for a Drug-Free World, "'I'll Just Try It Once.'" www.drugfreeworld.org.

## Chapter 3: A Highly Addictive Substance

15. *Economist*, "The Great American Relapse," November 22, 2014. www.economist.com.

16. Quoted in Libby Smith, "Heroin Use, Deaths on the Rise in Middle Class America," CBS Denver, October 21, 2013. http://denver.cbslocal.com.

17. Quoted in Michael Martinez, Ana Cabrera, and Sara Weis-feldt, "Denver Mom Survives Darkness of Prescription Drug Abuse Epidemic," CNN, August 27, 2014. www.cnn.com.

18. Beach, "It Happened to Me."

19. Elizabeth Hartney, "The Heroin High," Verywell, April 29, 2016. www.verywell.com.

20. Ed Byrne with J.F. Sargent, "5 Unexpected Things I Learned from Being a Heroin Addict," Cracked, February 16, 2014. www.cracked.com.

21. Quoted in Jason Cherkis, "Dying to Be Free," *Huffington Post*, January 28, 2015. http://projects.huffingtonpost.com.

22. Quoted in Nancy Eshelman, "Heroin Addict: 'I Don't Even Care About Myself. I Only Care About the Drug,'" PennLive, October 30, 2011. www.pennlive.com.

23. Brian Palmer, "Brain Changes in an Addict Make It Hard to Resist Heroin and Similar Drugs," *Washington Post*, February 17, 2014. www.washingtonpost.com.

24. Quoted in Scott Orr, "'Every Addict Has a Hole Inside Them That They're Trying to Fill,'" *Daily Courier*, March 11, 2016. www.dcourier.com.

25. Quoted in Your First Step, "Not What You Think: A Day in the Life of a Heroin Addict," May 19, 2014. http://yourfirststep .org.

26. Quoted in Your First Step, "Not What You Think."

27. Quoted in Joe Lawson, "Here's What It Felt Like When I Quit Heroin," Business Insider, February 5, 2014. www.business insider.com.

28. Quoted in Recovery Stories, "Journeys into and out of Heroin Addiction, Part 2." www.recoverystories.info.

29. Quoted in James Fisher, "Heroin-Fueled Crime Wave," Delaware Online, February 14, 2015. www.delawareonline.com.

## Chapter 4: The Challenges of Treatment and Recovery

30. Quoted in Ken Serrano, "Exclusive: Narcan Program Scores Success in First Month," *Asbury Park Press*, March 1, 2016. www.app.com.

31. Quoted in Ken Serrano, "Christie Praises Heroin Recovery Coaches," *Asbury Park Press*, March 22, 2016. www.app .com.

32. Quoted in Sarah T. Williams, "What's It Really Like to Withdraw from Heroin and Painkillers?," MinnPost, February 14, 2014. www.minnpost.com.

33. Quoted in Williams, "What's It Really Like to Withdraw from Heroin and Painkillers?"

34. Quoted in Sam Bonacci, "Ethan's Story, Part 3: 'Addiction Never Stops and I Will Live with This for the Rest of My Life, but There Are Ways to Maintain Control," MassLive, April 11, 2014. www.masslive.com.

35. Quoted in *PBS NewsHour*, "Why a Promising Heroin Addiction Treatment Is Unavailable in Many States," January 28, 2015. www.pbs.org.

## Chapter 5: Preventing Heroin Abuse

36. Quoted in Andy McDonald, "The Darkest Super Bowl Ad You Probably Never Saw," *Huffington Post*, February 1, 2015. www.huffingtonpost.com.

37. Quoted in Alfred Maskeroni, "This Bizarrely Bleak Super Bowl Ad About Heroin Was Even Darker than Nationwide's," *Adweek*, February 2, 2015. www.adweek.com.
38. National Conference of State Legislatures, "Drug Overdose Immunity and Good Samaritan Laws," April 12, 2016. www.ncsl.org.
39. Quoted in Kentucky Department of Public Advocacy, "Good Samaritan Immunity Saves Lives," June 26, 2015. http://dpa.ky.gov.
40. Quoted in *Huffington Post*, "Police Department Offers Heroin Addicts Amnesty, Treatment," August 14, 2015. www.huffingtonpost.com.
41. Quoted in *Huffington Post*, "Police Department Offers Heroin Addicts Amnesty, Treatment."
42. Quoted in Brian MacQuarrie, "Heroin Tide, Resolve Rise in Vermont," *Boston Globe*, April 6, 2015. www.bostonglobe.com.
43. Quoted in Gail Russell Chaddock, "How One State Turned Its 'Heroin Crisis' into a National Lesson," *Christian Science Monitor*, February 23, 2016. www.csmonitor.com.
44. Katharine Q. Seelye, "In Heroin Crisis, White Families Seek Gentler War on Drugs," *New York Times*, October 30, 2015. www.nytimes.com.
45. Quoted in *New York Times*, "Rethinking the Global War on Drugs," April 25, 2016. www.nytimes.com.
46. Abigail Hall, "The Drug War Failed in Afghanistan Too," *U.S. News & World Report*, July 20, 2015. www.usnews.com.

## American Society of Addiction Medicine (ASAM)

4601 N. Park Ave.
Upper Arcade, Suite 101
Chevy Chase, MD 20815-4520
phone: (301) 656-3920 • fax: (301) 656-3815
e-mail: e-mail@asam.org • website: www.asam.org

ASAM seeks to improve the quality of (and increase access to) addiction treatment, increase awareness of addiction, and support research and prevention efforts. Its website offers numerous articles, fact sheets, and other publications about painkiller and heroin addiction.

## Centers for Disease Control and Prevention (CDC)

1600 Clifton Rd.
Atlanta, GA 30329-4027
phone: (800) 232-4636
website: www.cdc.gov

America's leading health protection agency, the CDC seeks to promote health and quality of life by controlling disease, injury, and disability. Its website features numerous articles, fact sheets, and policy statements about prescription drug abuse, including heroin.

## DARE America (Drug Abuse Resistance Education)

9800 LaCienega Blvd., Suite 400
Inglewood, CA 90301
phone: (310) 215-0575
website: www.dare.org

The mission of DARE America is to provide young people with the information and skills they need to live their lives free from drugs and violence.

## Drug Enforcement Administration (DEA)

2401 Jefferson Davis Hwy.
Alexandria, VA 22301
phone: (202) 307-1000; toll-free: (800) 332-4288
website: www.dea.gov

The DEA is America's top federal drug law enforcement agency. Its website links to a separate site called Just Think Twice (www .justthinktwice.com) that is designed for teenagers and features fact sheets, personal experiences, and numerous publications about heroin and other drugs of abuse.

## Foundation for a Drug-Free World

1626 N. Wilcox Ave., Suite 1297
Los Angeles, CA 90028
phone: (818) 952-5260; toll-free: (888) 668-6378
e-mail: info@drugfreeworld.org • website: www.drugfreeworld.org

The Foundation for a Drug-Free World exists to empower young people with facts about drugs so they can make good decisions and live drug free. A wealth of information about heroin, painkillers, and other drugs is available on its website, including videos, fact sheets, and personal stories of teens who have fought addiction.

## Narcotics Anonymous (NA)

PO Box 9999
Van Nuys, CA 91409
phone: (818) 773-9999
website: www.na.org

Narcotics Anonymous is a global community–based group dedicated to helping addicts live their lives drug free. NA strives to deliver its message of hope to every addict in his or her own language and culture.

# National Institute on Drug Abuse (NIDA)

Office of Science Policy and Communications, Public Information and Liaison Branch
6001 Executive Blvd.
Room 5213, MSC 9561
Bethesda, MD 20892-9561
phone: (301) 443-1124
website: www.drugabuse.gov

NIDA works at advancing science on the causes and consequences of drug use and addiction, including heroin and opioids. It applies the knowledge gained to keep the public informed and improve individual and public health.

# Office of National Drug Control Policy

750 Seventeenth St. NW
Washington, DC 20503
phone: (800) 666-3332 • fax: (202) 395-6708
e-mail: ondcp@ncjrs.org • website: www.whitehouse.gov/ondcp

A component of the executive office of the president, the Office of National Drug Control Policy is responsible for directing the federal government's antidrug programs. A wealth of information about heroin can be brought up through the website's search engine.

# Partnership for Drug-Free Kids

352 Park Ave. South, 9th Floor
New York, NY 10010
phone: (212) 922-1560
website: www.drugfree.org

The Partnership for Drug-Free Kids focuses on helping families understand the changing drug landscape and provides parents direct support in dealing with young people's drug use, including heroin. The organization advocates for greater prevention efforts and improved access to treatment and recovery.

## Substance Abuse and Mental Health Services Administration (SAMHSA)

1 Choke Cherry Rd.
Rockville, MD 20857
phone: (877) 726-4727 • fax: (240) 221-4292
e-mail: SAMHSAInfo@samhsa.hhs.gov
website: www.samhsa.gov

The SAMHSA's mission is to reduce the impact of substance abuse and mental illness on America's communities. The site offers a wealth of information about substance abuse, and numerous publications related to heroin are available through its search engine.

## US Food and Drug Administration (FDA)

10903 New Hampshire Ave.
Silver Spring, MD 20993
phone: (888) 463-6332
website: www.fda.gov

The FDA is responsible for protecting the public health by assuring the safety, effectiveness, and security of drugs, biological products, medical devices, and the nation's food supply. Among the drugs it regulates are those used to treat heroin overdose and the symptoms associated with heroin withdrawal.

## Books

Michael Deibert, *In the Shadow of Saint Death: The Gulf Cartel and the Price of America's Drug War in Mexico*. New York: Lyons, 2014.

Humberto Fernandez and Therissa A. Libby, *Heroin: Its History, Pharmacology & Treatment*. Center City, MN: Hazelden, 2011.

Joani Gammill, *Painkillers, Heroin, and the Road to Sanity: Real Solutions for Long-Term Recovery from Opiate Addiction*. Center City, MN: Hazelden, 2014.

Tracey Helton Mitchell, *The Big Fix: Hope After Heroin*. Berkeley, CA: Seal, 2016.

Sam Quinones, *Dreamland: The True Tale of America's Opiate Epidemic*. New York: Bloomsbury, 2015.

## Internet Sources

Andrew Cohen, "How White Users Made Heroin a Public-Health Problem," *Atlantic*, August 12, 2015. www.theatlantic.com/politics/archive/2015/08/crack-heroin-and-race/401015.

Kenneth Craig, "Monthly Vivitrol Treatment Helps Fight Heroin Addiction," CBS News, January 19, 2016. www.cbsnews.com/news/vivitrol-vaccine-helps-fight-heroin-addiction.

Kelsey Dallas and Sandy Balazic, "How Heroin Made Its Way to the Suburbs," *Las Vegas Review-Journal*, February 19, 2015. www.reviewjournal.com/life/health/how-heroin-made-its-way-suburbs.

Brian Palmer, "Brain Changes in an Addict Make It Hard to Resist Heroin and Similar Drugs," *Washington Post,* February 17, 2014. www.washingtonpost.com/national/health-science/brain

-changes-in-an-addict-make-it-hard-to-resist-heroin-and-similar
-drugs/2014/02/14/dcc91c5e-9366-11e3-84e1-27626c5ef5fb
_story.html.

Barbara Tasch and Pamela Engel, "Mexican Cartels Now Have a 'Sophisticated Farm-to-Arm Supply Chain' for the US Heroin Trade," Business Insider, September 28, 2015. www .businessinsider.com/mexican-cartels-took-over-the-us-heroin -trade-2015-9.

## Websites

**Foundation for a Drug-Free World: The Truth about Heroin** (www.drugfreeworld.org/drugfacts/heroin.html). Devoted to providing the truth about drugs, this website features an excellent section on heroin. Included is an explanation of what heroin is, a capsule history of its origins, an explanation of its destructive effects, and statistics about its abuse worldwide.

**LiveScience** (www.livescience.com/51804-facts-about-heroin .html). This website includes many informative articles about heroin and heroin use, such as "10 Interesting Facts About Heroin." To access articles on the website about the most current research on heroin and opioids, the user should key in the word "heroin" in the search box.

**Neuroscience for Kids: Heroin** (https://faculty.washington.edu /chudler/hero.html). This is a brisk look at heroin, from the places where it is produced to how it is used and its effects on the user. The website also includes links to other sources about heroin.

**Village Behavioral Health** (www.villagebh.com/addiction/heroin /symptoms-signs-effects). This website provides a helpful overview of facts about heroin, including statistics, causes and risk factors for heroin abuse, and signs and symptoms of heroin abuse in teens.

# INDEX

# PICTURE CREDITS

# ABOUT THE AUTHOR

John Allen is a writer living in Oklahoma City.